NYC
NEW YORK CONNIVERS
FROM THE CREATOR OF *WHO SHOT THE SHERIFF?*

International Bestselling Author

John Alan Andrews

NEW YORK

CONNIVERS

THE N Y C SERIES

THE N Y CONNIVERS SERIES

Copyright © 2024 by John A. Andrews.

All rights reserved. Written permission must be secured from the publisher to use or reproduce any part of this book, except for brief quotations in critical reviews or articles.
Published in the U.S.A. by
Books That Will Enhance Your Life™

A L I - Andrews Leadership International
Entertainment Division®
Jon Jef Jam Entertainment®
www.JohnAAndrews.com
Cover Design: John A. Andrews
Cover Graphic Designer: A L I
Edited by: A L I
ISBN: 9798339308478

THE N Y CONNIVERS SERIES

"GOOD EVENING MYSTERY LOVERS...

WELCOME TO THE UNCANNY"

THE N Y CONNIVERS SERIES

UNTIL DEATH DO US PART

TABLE OF CONTENTS

CHAPTER ONE..5
CHAPTER TWO..8
CHAPTER THREE...11
CHAPTER FOUR..15
CHAPTER FIVE...20
CHAPTER SIX..23
CHAPTER SEVEN...26
CHAPTER EIGHT...30
CHAPTER NINE...34
CHAPTER TEN..37
CHAPTER ELEVEN..40
CHAPTER TWELVE..43
CHAPTER THIRTEEN..46
CHAPTER FOURTEEEN..49
CHAPTER FIFTEEN..52
CHAPTER SIXTEEN..57
CHAPTER SEVENTEEN..62
CHAPTER EIGHTEEN..66
CHAPTER NINETEEN..70
CHAPTER TWENTY..73
CHAPTER TWENTY-ONE..77
CHAPTER TWENTY-TWO..80
CHAPTER TWENTY-THREEE.....................................84
CHAPTER TWENTY-FOUR.......................................87
CHAPTER TWENTY-FIVE..90
CHAPTER TWENTY-SIX..93
CHAPTER TWENTY-SEVEN......................................96
CHAPTER TWENTY-EIGHT.....................................102
CHAPTER TWENTY-NINE......................................106
CHAPTER THIRTY..109
CHAPTER THIRTY-ONE..113
CHAPTER THIRTY-TWO..118
CHAPTER THIRTY-THREE......................................121
CHAPTER THIRTY-FOUR.......................................125
CHAPTER THIRTY-FIVE..129
CHAPTER THIRTY-SIX..135
CHAPTER THIRTY-SEVEN......................................138
CHAPTER THIRTY-EIGHT......................................143

THE N Y CONNIVERS SERIES

1

Brad and Beverly met while in Junior High and instantaneously fostered a relationship as childhood sweethearts. He was 15 then, and "Bev," as she preferred to be called, was entering puberty at age 13. Brad carried his father's name, Smith, and Bev her father's name - Tyson. Most of their peers dubbed them the duo "Bees" forever and ever. Like two peas in a pod, they rattled and rolled.

THE N Y CONNIVERS SERIES

Meanwhile, the girls from the jealous pack see Brad as a flirt and refer to him as B.S. He didn't mind their opinion of him one jiff. Instead, he strutted like a stud and spoke like Bradley the Numero Uno. Although he relished talking with other girls, he was content with being hitched to the hottest girl in school – Bev. That superiority caused the hairs on his chest to bud. The two Bees conveniently lived in the same Brooklyn neighborhood and shared the same school bus to and from Stuyvesant High – a multiracial school in the heart of Bedford-Stuyvesant.

It was like a fusion to see them getting off and onto the bus, even holding hands as they crossed the busy street sautéed with echoes of joy and laughter. Frankly, other girls at Stuyvesant High wished they had those feelings thrown their way, even by Romeo's magic wand.

Brad and Bev were so well-knitted at that early age. They even became adept at finishing each other's sentences whenever the opportunity arose in joint conversations. Yes. Two peas inside a pod scenario is an understatement for Bev and Brad conversing as they smiled from the inside out from the outside in. Beverly, though, carried a pompous swagger to let the other girls at Stuyvesant High know Brad Smith was her cuddle bunny, her lane her caboose, and that A-Train was beamingly speed down those H.S.

tracks warning: Please stay away from the platform's edge.

Upon graduation, their school principal, Trevor Matthews, in his congratulatory remarks, slipped up and said:

"I wish the best to Beverly and Brad – the two Bees in the beehive."

Their classmates even tried covering their mouths so as not to explode with laughter and revelry. During their principal, Mr. Matthews' instead of walking it back, smirked and continued with his closing remarks:

"Stuyvesant High is putting into relationships what the church and other institutions fail to accomplish. Here, it's not just about academics but about lifestyle."

Putting words of gold in pictures of silver, once again demonstrating his likeability for the Queen's English - his favorite cup of Tea. When he took his seat, students echoed chanting, "Stuyvesant! Stuyvesant! Stuyvesant!" coupled with a rhythmic standing ovation.

THE N Y CONNIVERS SERIES

2

Ten years later, in December 2007 Brad and Bev tied the knot. It was like an unconventional wedding. Littered with that High School class ex-undergraduates and their dates. Mr. Mathews lifted a toast to the groom and ironically recounted the story of the birds and the bees but in an enhanced mode:

"How the bees get nourished from and share the honeycomb..."

THE N Y CONNIVERS SERIES

Undoubtedly, he wanted to keep the days of Stuyvesant High monogrammed on the sleeves of Beverly Tyson and Brad Smith's minds. Consistent with putting his foot in his mouth, regrettably.

The Smiths and the Tysons' parents of the Bride and Groom were delighted to see their kids embark on this journey of Man and Wife. Beverly's dad, Mark Tyson, earned a living as an NYC stockbroker for over three decades —a good one, he was. Her mother, Esther, often referred to as "The Queen," was a stay-at-home mom who was undoubtedly there for Beverly when she came home from school.

Brad's parents owned a Taxi Medallion. His dad drove the yellow cab while Gracelyn, his wife, supervised at the Stuyvesant Public Library adorned in her Foster Grant spectacles. Brad gravitated to the stock market and, fortunately for himself, found a mentor in his father-in-law, Mark Tyson. Mark pushed him to complete his Series 6 exam on the first try.

After graduation, Beverly attended the Fashion Institute of Technology, where she honed her design skills. Developing a keen eye for fashion was her style. Her motto echoed:

"I am born to dress the world."

Bev could not only look at someone underneath those dark Ray-Ben sunglasses she wore most of the

time and instantaneously determine what outfit would look great on their frame but also innately possess the ability to design it. Her wedding gown was a classic example and bore her indelible signature.

This young couple loved Brooklyn immensely and eventually moved from Bedford Stuyvesant in the East to across town to Canarsie in the West. Their Ranch-style home was a dream come true and sat on two acres about a hundred yards from the Canarsie Trail. Unlike that of their neighbors, their home was gated. A gorgeous landscape, mainly Bev's epiphany and Brad's financial backing.

Inside their two-car garage, two fully loaded BMW autos were housed. Bev's name was tagged on hers, and Brad's was vice versa.

Bev loved horseback riding, and on early mornings, their two thoroughbreds, Britney and Beaver, neighed loudly from the barn in the backyard, a reminder to Brad and Bev it was time to wake up and go for a ride along that lengthy winding Canarsie Trail.

THE N Y CONNIVERS SERIES

3

It was approaching the eve of the couple's third anniversary when Brad received a phone call requesting he show up in Miami to facilitate the grand opening of his firm's brand new office. Sadly, the stockbroker assigned to those responsibilities, Noel Pendergrass, was released from his position both untimely and unexpectedly. So, instead of

THE N Y CONNIVERS SERIES

Planning a romantic setting with Bev, Brad embarked on this trip to Miami, and later, he tagged South Beach onto his itinerary — Yep, South Beach, Florida, of all places.

Back in 1964, South Beach, Florida, became very famous when Jackie Gleason brought his weekly variety series, The Jackie Gleason Show, to the area for taping, a rarity in the industry. Beginning in the late 1970s and continuing through the 1980s, that commune was used as a retirement community with moss ocean-front hotels and apartment buildings filled with elderly people living on small, fixed incomes. This period also saw the introduction of the "cocaine cowboys," drug dealers who used the area as a base camp for their illicit drug activities. Scarface, released in 1983, typifies this narcotic activity.

In addition, the television show Miami Vice used South Beach as a backdrop for much of its filming because of the area's raw and unique visual beauty. A somewhat recurring theme of early Miami Vice episodes were thugs and drug addicts barricading themselves in utterly run-down, almost ruin-like empty buildings. Only minor alterations had to be made for these scenes because many buildings in South Beach were in such poorly run-down

condition at the time. Even so, before the days of Miami Vice, South Beach was considered a very poor area with a very high crime rate.

Today, it is considered one of the wealthiest and most prosperous commercial areas on the beach. Recently, shows such as Repo have taken advantage of the backdrop and its immense cultural demographics. Despite this, poverty and crime still exist in some isolated places surrounding the area. But on the street, from evening until morning, people meet, mingle, and have a blast. In many ways, it resembles a city that doesn't sleep. Yet sensually upbeat.

The elongated palm trees supporting the roadside wave continuously ignited by the gentle, stiff breeze. The smell of exhaust fumes mixed with that salty air evaporates, creating a whiff derived like that from a Miami regatta.

South Beach, view towards east from 15th Street near Washington Avenue with the Loews, St. Moritz, and the Royal Palm Hotels in the background.

As previously alluded to, the South Beach section of Miami Beach is a major entertainment destination in both daytime and nightfall. It is bustling with hundreds of nightclubs, restaurants, boutiques, and hotels. Music and/or conversation reverberate from every structure, sidewalk, and vehicle. It is much a

THE N Y CONNIVERS SERIES

site to behold with exotic and local babes dressed to entice.

Unlike Brooklyn, New York, which has a strong West Indian and Latino population, South Beach is usually swarmed with both American and international tourists (mainly from Canada, Latin America, Europe, Israel, the Caribbean, and the United States), with some having permanent or second homes. A large number of European tourists also explain their influence on South Beach's lax and overall tolerance of the female monokini "aka topless" sunbathing, despite it being a public beach.

It was no happenstance that in December 2010, Brad Smith, a stockbroker from NYC (and still married to Beverly Tyson), met Tessa Santos, an escort, on the streets of South Beach, Miami, three years after tying the knot with his childhood sweetheart – the infamous Beverly Tyson from Stuyvesant High.

THE N Y CONNIVERS SERIES

4

Tessa, now in her late 20s was a remarkable sight, a knockout by any man's standard when it comes down to taste in a woman. She came in at 9.5 on a scale of one to ten. You can classify her as a woman to die for. Compared to Bev's beauty, Brad stepped up his game and taste for beautiful women. Brad, in his mid-40s, was rapidly climbing

THE N Y CONNIVERS SERIES

up the corporate ladder. He was buffed and fit. Tessa questioned Why he turned down offers to be featured on GQ's magazine cover. He responded: "Beverly wanted me to be just plain Brad, that's all." This did not sit too well with his new fling – Tessa. Who quibbled under her breath:
"How dare she? You are built like a doyen and should remain that way. I like the man I see in you." On the other hand, Brad's clients not only approved of his trading skills, but he did so as well. A double approval that certainly boosted his self-esteem. Simply put, he had what it took to land the right stocks for his clients, functioning as if he were the lead in that Boiler Room movie.

After their one-night rendezvous on that warm December night at the South Beach hotel suite, he opened up to Tessa on multiple fronts. Tessa drove him to the airport.

Brad caught an early morning flight headed north to NYC to make it on time for work. He held the keys to the office on the eighth floor of a high-rise commercial masterpiece overlooking Jackson Heights, Queens.

Unfortunately, that flight was delayed at least 45 minutes due to bad weather in Pennsylvania and the Carolinas. Once airborne, the pilot made up some time, thanks to a benevolent tailwind.

THE N Y CONNIVERS SERIES

When Brad arrived at LaGuardia Airport, he checked his watch and the big Rolex clock at LGA. Both timepieces reminded him that he was so late, and not even a miracle could turn back the hands of time. The only advantage he now had was to get there earlier rather than later.

So, he caught a taxi and verbally navigated the cab driver through shortcuts, which got him to the Firm at 9:20 AM, some 20 minutes after his scheduled arrival time. Although he could slide in minutes before the bell, his preparation lacked luster and authentic quotes.

Trading on Wall Street was huge that morning. Stocks plummeted. The firm could not manage without its stellar trader helming proficiently.

Not only were his co-workers waiting in the first-floor lobby for someone with the keys, but his boss, who still had a vacancy to fill, also showed up unexpectedly without his keys.

For Brad, on all counts, this was not looking good for someone known to run things and run them well. Upon his arrival, his co-workers were shocked regarding his late onset. Brad felt as though the rug was slipping away from underneath him. Had he left Miami on Sunday night as his firm had scheduled, he would have made it back to NYC before Monday's workday.

THE N Y CONNIVERS SERIES

He was always on time, five out of five, 52 weeks a year. So, he had some serious explaining to do. His alibi placed him on a later trip, and the whole flight delay situation compounded it, he said.

They bought into his alibi, but Brad carried a different aura, and they smelled it immediately. The fumes were toxic, like diesel exhaust. That manly innocence that he'd previously protracted had not only taken a back seat but moved underneath the trunk. They sensed his guilt and raised concerns in their minds.

"Brad, I'll cover your shift."

Voiced one of his co-workers.

"Thanks. I've got this."

Brad responded proudly as he shuffled papers on his desk. The day went by swiftly amidst the office chaos and confusion. Brad loaded up on coffee as if it were a chain-smoking episode.

Internally, his mind rattled like the clattering head of a rattlesnake. Even so, externally, Brad had lost his venom for trading as he had previously - directly in the bullseye. His clients were misdirected in trade decisions, and this pissed them off.

The stocks tumbled further, creating yet another upset. No one knew why they did, but Brad sensed himself as being placed in the center of it all. Besides downing all that caffeine, he was smitten with the

THE N Y CONNIVERS SERIES

idea that if Bev would also sense that vibe felt by his co-workers and clients, he could become dead, dead meat.

Soon, it was time for Brad to return home to his wife Beverly after that sensual and steamy South Beach encounter. Would he have to confess that he was a categorical cheat?

THE N Y CONNIVERS SERIES

5

Upon arriving home, Beverly,, on the other hand, was happy to see her husband Brad, although their third-anniversary merriment was an absolute wash. She prepared him a nice meal accented with a bottle of his favorite wine. They ate together and later fell asleep in each other's arms. Like it's said:
"What happens in Vegas stays in Vegas!"

THE N Y CONNIVERS SERIES

Brad was prepared to let what happened in South Beach stay indefinitely in South Beach. If it boiled up and spilled over, he was ready to blame it on the airline, his boss, and the firm. The latter at the deepest level, which he felt had much to do with him missing their third anniversary. Even so, he could not get Tessa Santos off his mind. She lingered and dangled like the odor of sweet-smelling perfume.

That night, my mind weighed heavily over matte. Brad tossed and turned, consumed with the haunting memories of being assessed. It seemed demonic, as Tessa possessed his mind, heart, soul, and even his adulterated sixth sense.

Morning came, and he prepared to leave for work much earlier than usual. Beverly asked:

"What was wrong with you last night you tossed and turned like you were aboard a ship sailing on rough seas in the Atlantic?"

"It must have been the wine, honey. Where did you fetch that bottle?"

Brad asked.

"It's the same wine, Brad. It did not change. You were the one who put it in the cellar, remember? Sex was different, though. A little …, Were you…? Did you…?" "It's not what you are thinking. Well, if it's not that wine, it must have been a serious relapse

THE N Y CONNIVERS SERIES

from the turbulence of that flight. I felt that airplane was going to land in the swamps of New Jersey."
Said Brad as he kissed Beverly on her lips and headed for his BMW.
"You left your planner! This has never happened, Brad."
Said Beverly, running towards the door. She retrieved the planner and handed it to him.
"Thanks, Bev!"
Brad boarded his car and speedily headed off to work. Shortly after that, Beverly got dressed in sweat and left the house. She boarded her BMW and followed him as a P.I. for miles until he arrived at the firm in Jackson Heights.
Satisfied, Beverly turned back and headed to her job at the Manhattan Fashion District. Ironically, it was a busy day at the designer's warehouse. Bev dropped the ball on multiple appointments. Her day was simultaneously turned upside down. Luckily, Mrs. Barnes, her assistant, stood in the gap and salvaged...

THE N Y CONNIVERS SERIES

6

After that day, Beverly phoned Brad mainly to check up on him. Brad told her he was doing fine and not to worry. As soon as they hung up the phone, like clockwork, Tessa phoned Brad. Tessa reminisced about how much she had missed him and was very much into him. She reminded him of their wonderful time together that

night on South Beach. Also, he seemed intoxicated by her brand of champagne - Crystal.

"I can't wait to see you again...my desire is your fav." She reiterated.

On this phone conversation, Brad could not help but reminisce about the unconventional time they enjoyed that night in South Beach. They also talked about the possibility of intensifying the fire coexisting between them. The fuel was hers to pour... It seemed when it came down to Tessa that Brad was walking on clouds favored by the Latter Rain, but with Bev in this triangular relationship, he was digging deep underground tunnels.

Brad left work very early that evening and headed home, exasperated.

Beverly arrived home late that evening before hanging out with some of her girlfriends. The girl who talks like a clique placed Brad's behavioral flip centerstage. They filled up her tank until it overflowed.

When Bev arrived at the house, something was in the air, and her intuition told her it wasn't euphoric. Bev entered the house tentatively, though. Brad's wedding band and an accompanying manila envelope were on the dining table. Beverly choked up. She teared up.

THE N Y CONNIVERS SERIES

Anyway, she mustered up enough courage to open the envelope. Inside, she found not only a note stating Brad wanted his exit but also a stack of divorce papers to be signed. Even so, portions of the decree were redacted.
"What the heck is he trying to cover up?"
Beverly opined in her self-talk.
The tears welled up more than ever in Beverly's eyes and then dripped rapidly down her face. Troubled unwittingly on mixed thoughts of contesting and terminating the good thing she thought they had going on now became her dominant obsession.

THE N Y CONNIVERS SERIES

7

Brad goes MIA again. That weekend, he elopes with Tessa. While back in NYC, Bev consulted with her divorce attorney. To make his plan feasible, Brad asks his boss, Michael James, to transfer him from the NYC office to the partnering Firm in Miami. Michael attended Stuyvesant High and witnessed firsthand the birth of Brad and Bev's relationship.

THE N Y CONNIVERS SERIES

"Is Bev on board with your new decision?"
Michael probed.
"That's a work in progress."
Said Brad, with Michael sticking a pin as the phone rang. Brad promptly answered it. Anyway, his boss was obliged despite Brad's conversational cliffhanger. He knew that wherever Brad landed, it would increase the bottom line for the firm — one week after arriving in South Beach, Miami. Brad reconfigured himself into the workforce as a new Floridian stockbroker with a chic Penthouse office.

He was close to Tessa and at this point, that proximity mattered most to him. Tessa was elated that her newfound lover Brad Smith had not only decided to elope but to bring his employ to her neighborhood. On the other hand, Beverly felt Brad could have been more of a man; by discussing the situation with her but he chose not. He resisted closure. Instead, he left Bev sitting anxiously without full disclosure.

Disgusted with herself, Bev called Brad at work when the news leaked: he had headed south.

"Brad, why are you doing this to me and our relationship?"
Bev queried.

Brad responded:

THE N Y CONNIVERS SERIES

"I don't want to mess with your feelings. I want out... With my move to Florida and the new promotion...Bev, this relationship will be strenuous on both of us...the organization...you up north and me down south...you know what I mean?" "No. I don't know what you mean...whatever happened to the compromising Brad? The Bradley Smith who held my hand as we crossed the street?" Bev asked.

Bev did not buy into his Kool-Aid, cockamamie, half-baked story. He could not even keep his thoughts straight. Your alibi is unleavened, half-baked, and unproperly served up... evidence your yeast lost its bounce."

Bev added rhetorically.

Bev endeavored that she wouldn't sign those papers to let him off that twisted hook from which he dangled. She phoned her lawyer and asked him to pump the brakes. Bev was content with sitting on the ...Papers, even if her fence-sitting hurt more than a migraine headache and toothache emanating from a wisdom tooth.

By this time, though, she was gradually getting her confidence back. Subsequently, she thought it out thoroughly, preceded by "click," and aborted the phone call.

THE N Y CONNIVERS SERIES

THE FOLLOWING DAY, while Bev was at work, Brad conveniently took the day off and flew back to NYC unannounced. He surveyed and then entered the house. He rummaged, packed some of his belongings, and loaded up a rented SUV, wanting to depart the premises urgently.

Brad still found himself stuck under the driver's seat. Not because the automobile wouldn't start but because his mind, heart, and soul told him that with Bev, he still belonged. As he pursued the relinquishing of those thoughts, he glanced through the rear-view mirror and saw an elderly couple strolling down the street arm in arm. Recounting those days when he and Bev were so much in love, he couldn't dispel.

His shoulders are now weighty as he rid himself of doubt, dismay, and decay. Brad cranked up the engine and departed Southernly on his way.

THE N Y CONNIVERS SERIES

8

Bev arrived home several hours later. As she pulled into the driveway, her intuition told her something else had gone amiss. As she entered the house, she noticed Brad's favorite necktie lying on the living room floor. In her quest for more discovery, she ignored the necktie. Entering the bedroom, she realized Brad evacuated his entire

wardrobe from the abode except for that "fell-by-the way" necktie. Bev chose not to pick the clothing accessory off the floor. To her, tidying up had lost its momentum.

That night, she tossed and turned in bed as if she were now sailing on those rough seas.

The following morning, Beaver, and Britney, the two horses in the stable, took their wake-up call to multiple decibels. They neighed like it was the new norm. This caught her attention at a penetrative level. Bev jumped out of bed. I opened the window and discovered the thoroughbreds in disarray. She briskly got dressed in her sweats and hurried to the stable. There, she noticed the hay intended for their nourishment tossed all over their dwelling. Bev served them some fresh hay, returned to the house, grabbed an apple, and devoured it. After which, she mounted onto Beaver, and Britney followed in tow, led by a rope.

An hour later, they returned home, and both horses were stable.

It's obvious Bev was still carrying some extra burden on her mind, tangled in this web of autonomy.

She boarded her BMW and headed through the neighborhood, discombobulated. At the newsstand, she fetched the early morning paper and perused... Nothing on its front page mattered; not even the

THE N Y CONNIVERS SERIES

centerfold served as a hook to go shop till she dropped. Instead, she sprinted to the horse racing section and placed bets on her predictable winners. Speedy Gonzales captured her interest. A horse many betters claimed could one day capture first place in every race it entered into.
When Bev and Brad were together, Brad would sometimes take her to the races.
"Boy, did he bet on some losers? Like Hasty Hastings and Relentless James."
She said under her breath. I would bet on some losers. She recalled as he placed her bets. However, Bev never indulged at the time. She had instead accompanied Brad mainly for moral support. Rebellion would have turned her into a Jinks. However, today, she had identified the projected winners and headed off to the Belmont Racetrack. Her palms sweated, perspiration beaded down her face as she careened the car from Canarsie, along the Belt Parkway East, and on into Queens.
That look of derision, though, gleamed in her eyes like the pounce of a tiger despite being buried under a landslide of fear, guilt, and solitude. She depleted the box of facial tissues before pulling up at the parking lot at Belmont several minutes later. With her chest protruding and head tilted high, she claimed the vacant seat on the masculine-laden front

THE N Y CONNIVERS SERIES

row. "Bang!" …and the racing began. Unfortunately for Bev, though, she lost on her first bets in the margin of that day's Racing column at Belmont. Speedily, it landed third, and she had him all marked up at second. Yet, she was confident she picked the winner.

Among other bets, Bev unanimously placed bets on Speedy Gonzalez, coming in second and winning all the multiple races in which the horse performed. Her total wins at Belmont that day equaled over $1.2M. The most significant amount ever won in a one-day tally at Belmont.

As if hanging on a Cloud of Favor, Beverly rushed to the Nail Salon and pampered herself with a Manicure, Pedicure, and pluck of the eyebrows.

On the way home, she made a detour to the neighborhood's Gun Shop, where she purchased her first weapon, a 45 semi-automatic.

Later that morning, she boarded the Chinese Bus heading south to Florida.

One day later, she arrived promptly in South Beach, Miami.

THE N Y CONNIVERS SERIES

9

That same evening, over dinner, Tessa told Brad she glimpsed Beverly at the mall and consequently felt threatened by her. "What was she doing at the mall in Miami?" Brad asked. "Not sure. She was wearing dark glasses and seemed weaving through a crowd towards me. I made a detour and eventually eluded her. Still, later, I saw her again. I don't trust your ex. My sixth sense tells

me she's up to something nefarious in nature. Why the heck was she stalking me?"
Tessa asked in disgust.

Those relayed series of events got to Brad. Upsetting him so much that he couldn't even enjoy the meal. His glass of champagne turned from chilled to room temperature. He spent most of his time consoling his newfound love -Tessa. Try as hard as he did; there remained a residue of fear in Tessa regarding being stalked by Beverly Tyson on her home turf. So much that hither-fore, whenever Bev's name was mentioned, Tessa displayed a double sense of uneasiness.

Tessa, meaning "Test-her," was born and raised in NYC and still had an affinity with the Big Apple. She loved wearing very little in the summer and layering up in the frigid winter. Since moving to Miami, her wardrobe became one-dimensional.

As a surprise, the next weekend Brad treated her to a NYC getaway. Tessa went shopping and supplanted her wardrobe for the New York spring weather. She was stoked to return to the fully awake city after ten years.

"New York, here I come!"
She echoed.

THE N Y CONNIVERS SERIES

Those New York pleasantries included Broadway shows, Junior's cheesecake, and bar hopping—commonalities that bode well for the duo.

THE N Y CONNIVERS SERIES

10

Ironically, on that same weekend, tracing a 911 call by neighbors, Detectives Jamie Johnson and Jonathan Hobbs arrived at Beverly Tyson's house. It was obvious by the broken glass on the front door someone had broken in, or some form of vandalism had occurred. Even though, at this point, it was still speculative.

THE N Y CONNIVERS SERIES

As the detectives entered the house probingly, Beverly Tyson lay motionless in a bloodbath,, a necktie tightly clenched in her left fist. Multiple gunshot wounds to the head discourse - tragedy. Behind her corpse, a gun resembling a 45 semi-automatic weapon, which she bought at the gun shop and took on her Miami pursuit, was discovered.

To the detectives, it smelled like suicide. However, it also tasted like homicide. To the cops, the man's tie soaked in blood and fastened in her hand-loomed large, indicating a man or someone stronger than the victim could have conducted the murder proceeded by a struggle. Plus, the abandoned necktie. Neighbors reportedly had seen Brad dress in that necktie. It was his fav.

After the crime scene was secured, Det. Hobbs and Jamison followed an anonymous tip to the Hampton Inn outside LaGuardia Airport. Announcing themselves outside room 515, Brad opened the door to much surprise.

After probing his itinerary, the detectives entered. Brad and Tessa were packing for their return trip, heading back to Miami via LGA.

Subsequently, they were detained, questioned further, and arrested by Hobbs and Jamison on suspicion of murdering Beverly Tyson - Smith. Days later, it was determined the only prints lifted from

THE N Y CONNIVERS SERIES

that murder weapon matched Beverly Tyson's. However, Brad's necktie soaked in blood, and the broken glass pane on the front door of the house led NYC detectives to believe a whiff of homicide permeated. Plus, they recovered the partially redacted divorce decree bearing the fingerprints of both Brad Smith and Tessa Santos and signed by Brad Smith. Subsequently, Brad Smith and Tessa Santos stayed in prison, marking time.

THE N Y CONNIVERS SERIES

11

While Brad and Tessa remained in prison without bail. The case in which they were charged was gaining enormous public empathy not only within the media but from those gossiping and eavesdropping neighbors. The media reasoned Brad and Tessa had clear motives to murder Beverly Tyson. Brad, most outlets claimed

couldn't get the divorce he so desperately wanted from Beverly to marry Tessa, so he murdered his wife, Beverly. Additionally, Bev was loaded; she owned a strong insurance policy with over a million dollars going to her beneficiary upon her death. Plus, on the day before she was murdered, she had purchased a gun, which, according to evidence, took her life.

Days before her death, she walked away with a purse of over $1M from the Belmont Racetrack in bets on Speedy Gonzales. The couple had no kids. So, Brad, by default, was deemed the sole beneficiary. Additionally, one day before Bev was murdered, she talked with her banker and sat up an appointment for the next day to dissolve the joint bank account that she opened with Brad.

Sadly, she was gunned down one day prior. The home on two acres was still in the couple's name pending mediation. However, Beverly chose to put all divorce proceedings on hold. Anyway, it's clear, based on what was known thus far, that every asset she owned would go to Brad if she died before him.

It was also speculated and spun in the media: Brad could have shared information about Bev's assets with Tessa. If he did, that knowledge could have certainly prompted Tessa to orchestrate the murder of Beverly Tyson-Smith. In the meantime, their

THE N Y CONNIVERS SERIES

neighbors conversed about how insecure the marriage looked from the start. They claimed:

"No matter what the couple had going for them romantically, Bev always looked like a loner." Some even took pictures of Bev when she rode her horse Beaver to the Trail and the other horse – Britney followed in tow. Even though their interpretation of the facts could have been considerably skewed, they held on to what they witnessed and felt they had clear evidence to support their discernment of the couple's twisted, on the razor-thin edge relationship. Consequently, no one was privy to the foregoing information, as both accused were still incarcerated and pending trial in the Southern District of New York courthouse.

THE N Y CONNIVERS SERIES

12

Meanwhile, Jury selection was underway for this well-publicized upcoming trial. The eclectic pool of jurors assembled eventually dwindled down to 12 and 5 alternates. The makeup of The Twelve included 6 men and 6 women, 2 from the LBGT community - 1 gay person and 1 Lesbian. Juror # 1 and Head Juror – a 32-year-

THE N Y CONNIVERS SERIES

old Lesbian and graduate of Yale Law School with a BA in Law and Liberal Arts. Outspoken and driven, with a desire to lead authoritatively.

Juror # 2 – an elderly Caucasian man. Old enough to be the father of the victim Beverly Tyson-Smith. His tenure before retirement landed him in the Financial District and Wall Street. He possessed a keen eye for numbers.

Juror # 3 – an elderly woman, who spent the last 30 years serving as a Librarian with the New York City Libraries. Although senior in years, she proved to be what some may call a smart Alec or in the case of a woman a smart Alice.

Juror # 4 – a man of color and a retiree from the NYPD. One who has just about seen everything. Not only in the lives of civilians but also his peers.

Juror # 5 – a millennial, gay and very articulate persona. Also, I am a graduate of Columbia School of Law. He epitomizes Mayor Pete Buttigieg and could be his body double.

Juror # 6 – a train conductor and Latino woman from the MTA, who speaks very fluent English. However, when she drops her Spanish it could be very deep.

Juror # 7 – an African American woman who has roots grounded in the advertising industry. She's stylish and very articulate.

THE N Y CONNIVERS SERIES

Juror # 8 – a man from a construction employer. He does not only wear the hard hat but as the father of three sons and three daughters, he's seasoned with that hard hat-wearing persona.

Juror # 9 – a Latino used car salesman from Long Island. A fast-talking specimen. Has the ability to con you into buying a lemon.

Juror # 10 – a long-bearded Indian college Professor. He comes across as an intellectual who spouts his dialect at a deep sophisticated level.

Juror # 11 – a female Hairstylist from Brooklyn. Feisty as they come. She relishes wearing HBO – Hair Belonging to Others.

Juror # 12 - a female RN with New York Hospitals. A woman who believes she can fix everything. With detectives, Jonathan Hobbs in a quest to earn his stripes and Jamie Johnson a cop from the streets of Harlem, involved in this case the stakes were expected to be a very high courtroom drama.

THE N Y CONNIVERS SERIES

13

Representing the government: District Attorneys out of the Southern District of New York, Douglas Tibbs and Claudia Mendez were poised to proceed with this double-defendants murder trial. Mendez, a stern Me-Too movement activist, while Douglas Tibbs, her dull-witted sidekick – is adept at shadowing and deflecting. Very confident they have a strong case.

THE N Y CONNIVERS SERIES

Even though one foot seemed to be resting in suicide territory and the other in homicide terrain. These two DAs were set to dispute most of the spin webbed by the media and trumped up as suicide. They opined Brad Smith and Tessa Santos resided at center stage in this murder debacle and should be found guilty. Although the word on the streets was: Murderous, evidence looked scanty. Mendez and Tibbs were willing to prove it: if all else fails circumstantial evidence with whatever they can conjure up.

As additional evidence in this case surfaced, it became clear the DAs were prepared to drill down deep and wide, even tapping into the couple's finances by subpoenaing records from their Banker, as well as dragging in Brad Smith's realtor to testify. They debated Brad Smith's necktie and placed him at the murder scene: possibly in a struggle with his wife Beverly.

Plus, it was determined: Tessa's DNA was all over those divorce papers, more so the envelope. Technically, Brad and Tessa's trip to NYC that weekend, if they had nothing to do with the murder, surely gave the impression they were premeditatively linked to it like a hand in glove.

On the other hand, the defense headed by Samuel Taliaferro and Calista Cochran was prepared to prove it a suicide. Why? Bev felt she had lost

THE N Y CONNIVERS SERIES

everything when Brad walked, so she didn't want to have to face life alone.

"It was enough for Bev to frequently take both horses to the trail and only ride on one horseback." Stated one neighbor who preferred to remain anonymous.

Why did Bev resort to buying a gun after Brad said he wanted out of the marriage? Did she then embrace suicidal tendencies, or did she entertained the desire to kill Brad, his girlfriend and then kill herself? The tenacious Samuel Taliaferro and We are in this together Calista Cochran was ready to tee off in the courtroom.

THE N Y CONNIVERS SERIES

14

Journalists not only argued those forgoing questions but spun the theories like a sleeping tap on Cable TV. Exactly two weeks after jury selection the trial was set to begin. Neighbors of the murdered Beverly Tyson - Smith, as well as the media, swarmed the steps of the Southern District Court of New York. The media pressed in a quest for

any audio and/or late-breaking news video footage to facilitate their news cycle. Meanwhile, microphones mounted on a lectern staged on the steps of the courthouse lay in waiting. The neighbors? Most of them showed up to lend support to the friends and family of Beverly.

Inside the courtroom, the gold-plated name tag on the Judge's desk reads The Honorable Claude Thomas. Court attendees saunter in. The Defense team made up of Samuel Taliaferro and Calista Cochran were first to enter. They halted in the aisle and then huddled on the right side in front of the Judge's bench.

The prosecution then ambled in briskly. Seating themselves on the opposite side of the defense. Helmed by Claudia Mendez and Douglas Tibbs, the duo chit-chatted, followed by an exchange of dialog with one of the attending court clerks.

Finally, in walked Brad Smith and Tessa Santos escorted by uniformed courtroom officials. They occupied vacant seats on the same row as the defense. The case was set to begin, except the Judge was not yet in his seat behind the bench. Brad glanced across at the lectern and then whispered something in Tessa's ear. Tessa then scanned the room.

THE N Y CONNIVERS SERIES

Across the way, Beverly's Mom and Dad sat next to the prosecutors. Bev's mom choked up and opened her purse from which she removed some facial tissues and dried the tears now flowing down her cheeks. Mark, Bev's dad put his hands around his wife Esther's shoulder and consoled her sympathetically. Brad's parents ambled in and sat on the row behind their son. Tessa's parents did vice versa.

Suddenly, the Bailiff echoed:

"All rise!"

Inside Brad's mind resonated: lights, action, camera. Judge Thomas in his black robe enters from the back and inhabits his black chair at the bench. As everyone else grabbed their seats: A loud scream crescendos' from inside the courtroom. Eyes are now locked in on Bev's younger sister Alecia Tyson. She becomes uncontrollable. The bailiff steps over and meticulously unruffled the disruptive relative.

THE N Y CONNIVERS SERIES

15

After some brief opening remarks from the prosecution and the defense, the prosecution called their first witness Detective Jonathan Hobbs "aka Hans." District Attorney Claudia Mendez stepped up to the lectern.
"Mr. Hobbs, what is your current profession?"
She asked.
"I'm a detective with the NYPD."
Answers Det. Hobbs.

THE N Y CONNIVERS SERIES

"How long have you been with the NYPD, Detective Hobbs?"

Asks the Prosecution.

"This December will be 5 years since I began my employ."

Responds Detective Hobbs.

"Are you a good cop or a bad cop?"

"Objection!"

Yells Taliaferro.

"Objection overruled!"

Barked the judge.

"Mr. Hobbs where were you on the evening of April 13?"

Asks Claudia Mendez.

"I was orchestrating at a speed trap along the Belt Parkway and Rockaway Avenue with my partner Jamie Johnson."

Says Hobbs.

"And what happened?" "When we received and responded to a 911 call regarding gunshots heard in the chic Canarsie neighborhood. The call led us to 713 N. Seaview Avenue, a Ranch House. We could tell by the broken glass on the front door. The door was still slightly ajar. Glass fragments saturated the entrance to the house. Entering, we noticed a woman's body saturated in blood. In her left hand, a colorful necktie tightly grasped.

THE N Y CONNIVERS SERIES

My partner, Detective Johnson rushed to see if she was still breathing. She tried CPR…nothing! She tried again, to no avail. Next to the woman's body, a 45 semi-automatic pointing towards the entrance. Her bleeding head wounds seemed to be bullet inflicted. The stench of gunfire filled the atmosphere."
"What else did you notice?"
Asked the DA.
"Blood layering most of that living room floor."
Said Det. Hobbs.
"What did you and your partner do?"
Asked Claudia Mendez.
"We alerted our dispatchers and secured the crime scene with tape."
"And then?"
Asked the DA.
"A man showed up attempting to enter the crime scene. We pushed back. He informed us the victim's husband was apparently staying across town at the Airport Hampton Inn. We departed the crime scene based on his tip. Moments later we pulled up outside the hotel, went inside checked the guest list and moments later we knocked on room 515."
"And then what happened?"
"A man who we later learned to be Brad Smith; the victims' husband answered the door. He asked what

we wanted. We told him there was a murder in the neighborhood and we wanted to ask him some questions. He said come on in."

"And then what happened?"

"We entered the room."

"And what happened as you and your partner entered?"

Asked the Prosecution.

"We told him Beverly Smith was murdered and asked if he knew who might have killed her. He said that's my wife, and immediately began to sob. We told him we wanted to ask him a few questions in conjunction with her murder. We were then introduced to Tessa Santos, who was also in the room busily engaged in packing. They seemed hurried. Brad disclosed they could be late for the flight. Even so, he entertained our questioning."

"What did you do then?"

Asked the Prosecutor.

"We detained and arrested Brad Smith and Tessa Santos."

Says Hobbs.

"Did you know Brad Smith and Tessa Santos prior to their arrests?"

Asked the DA.

THE N Y CONNIVERS SERIES

"No. I had never met them. Not sure my partner did either." Said Det. Hobbs. Claudia Mendez facilitates a list of experiments.
"Is this experiment - # 1, the necktie you discovered clenched in the victim's left hand?"
Asks Mendez.
"Yes. It is."
Says Hobbs.
"Is this handgun, experiment # 2 the gun you saw next to the victim's body?"
Asked the DA.
The detective seems unsure. Judge urges.
"Look at it closely now, Det. Hobbs."
Hobbs responds:
"It does bear some resemblance of the gun recovered at the crime scene."
Judge Thomas interjects:
"Are you finished with your questioning Counsel?"
"Yes, your honor.'
Claudia Mendez responds and takes her seat. Judge Thomas yells! "
Mr. Taliaferro, your witness."

THE N Y CONNIVERS SERIES

16

Samuel Taliaferro steps over to the lectern and engages Det. Jonathan Hobbs. "Det. Jonathan Hobbs, did you know Brad Smith when he attended Stuyvesant High along with Beverly Smith, then Tyson?" "Your honor, I move to strike. That is irrelevant." Says DA Mendez. "You may answer the question, Detective!"
Says Judge Thomas.

THE N Y CONNIVERS SERIES

"No. I did not know him then."
Says Hobbs.
"Detective, according to your written statement, you indicated you received a tip from a neighbor which led you to the hotel where Mr. Brad Smith was staying? Is that correct."
Asks Taliaferro.
"That's correct."
"Who provided you with such a tip?"
Asks Taliaferro.
"Objection!"
Yells Claudia Mendez.
"Objection overruled!"
Yells Judge Thomas.
"Again, I ask you, Detective, who provided you with the tip?"
Taliaferro waits for the shoe to drop.
"Noel Pendergrass."
"Noel Pendergrass? ...And what affiliation has Noel Pendergrass with my clients, Brad Smith, and Tessa Santos?"
Asks Taliaferro.
"I've later learned Brad Smith worked together with Pendergrass at the firm. Not sure if he knew Tessa Santos."
Says Pendergrass.

THE N Y CONNIVERS SERIES

"Detective, in your written statement you failed to mention who provided you with the tip. Was that done on purpose?"
Asks Taliaferro.
"No. At that point when Pendergrass volunteered that info, I was more concerned with tracking down the murderer than with the informer's true identity."
Says Hobbs.
"Do you think it borders on incompetence when a law enforcement officer omits important facts from an oral or written testimony?"
Asks Taliaferro.
"I wouldn't consider it incompetence?"
Says Hobbs.
"Would you say it's negligence?"
Presses the defense.
"No."
Says Hobbs.
"Would you say it was choice evidentiary neglect on your part?"
Asks Taliaferro.
"No. It wasn't."
"None of the aforementioned?"
Asks Taliaferro.
"Neither."
Says Detective Hobbs.

THE N Y CONNIVERS SERIES

"Did Mr. Pendergrass inform you at that time or thereafter that he participated in a love triangle with the couple, and that he had on one night visited their home while the couple was intoxicated?" "Your honor, I move to strike!"
Shouts Claudia Mendez.
Judge Thomas summons a sidebar conference promptly. Brad Smith, amazed sits up straight, then resorts to sitting on the edge of his seat. Likewise, many other court attendees are unnerved by that line of questioning. In particular Beverly Tyson's relatives. Tessa affixes her arm to Brad's right arm.
The two attorneys return. Taliaferro takes his seat as well. As if forgetting something he stands and addresses:
"You stated previously after questioning my clients, then you detained them."
"Yes."
"Detective, when you detained my clients, could you describe their demeanor?"
"Yes. They were both remorseful."
Says Hobbs. "About what?"
Asks Taliaferro.
"I'm not...sure."
States Hobbs.

THE N Y CONNIVERS SERIES

"Your honor I have no further questions at this point." The court then called Detective Jamie Johnson. Johnson corroborated much of what her partner Jonathan Hobbs testified. However, during cross-examination Taliaferro asked her:
"If she knew there was a triangular relationship between Pendergrass, Brad and Beverly Smith."
She said she was not privy to any such information.
At this point, the court went on recess. The buzz between attendees heading out of the courtroom crescendo. The pow-wow leaks, it escalates, having much to do with the triangular line of questions. Keeping his distance is a witness for the prosecution not yet called – Noel Pendergrass.

THE N Y CONNIVERS SERIES

17

During the break, Noel Pendergrass wind up at the prosecution's office a few blocks from the courthouse. While the defense huddled at their nearby office. Claudia Mendez and Douglas Tibbs begin to press Noel Pendergrass.
"What is your affiliation with Brad and the late Beverly Tyson - Smith? You have not yet been called

THE N Y CONNIVERS SERIES

to testify but we want to save ourselves the embarrassment or any element of surprise. Those jurors look like they are the cream of the NYC crop."
Says Claudia Mendez and continues.
"We keep hearing about this Triangular Love Affair." "Triangular?"
Asks Pendergrass.
"Yes. Triangular! What was your outside-of-work relationship with that couple?"
Asks Douglas Tibbs. "Nothing."
Says Pendergrass.
"We need you to think hard. Recall!"
Says Tibbs.
"There's only one incident I can recall."
States Pendergrass. "…And what's that?"
Asks Tibbs. Mendez is listening carefully.
"One night after the news broke that the firm where I worked with Brad at the time, was expanding their operation to Miami, Florida. I heard through the grapevine: Brad was targeted to helm this firm. We later went out for drinks. Brad invited Beverly. After multiple rounds, I sensed Brad and Beverly had too much to drink. She was clawing all over him. I offered to drive them home. Brad refuted."
Pendergrass reflects.
"Go on!"

THE N Y CONNIVERS SERIES

Says Claudia Mendez. Pendergrass continues, "Beverly nibbled on his ear and asked him to take me up on the offer. I told them they can pick up their car in the morning. That night I drove the couple to their house. Beverly during most of the trip argued with Brad about an alleged affair. No name was called. I sensed she was labeling Brad as a cheat."
"And what did you say?"
"Nothing."
"That's all?"
Asks Claudia Mendez.
"Who was this third party in question?"
Asked Mendez.
"That name was never disclosed."
Says Pendergrass.
"That's all you want to tell us?"
"Yes. That is all?"
Says Noel Pendergrass.
"Were you in any way attracted to Beverly Tyson - Smith?" "Not at all." "Why didn't you tell us about this?"
Asks Mendez.
Noel Pendergrass has had enough. He storms out closing the door behind himself.
"We're… you know what?"
Says Mendez.

THE N Y CONNIVERS SERIES

"What if they were to milk this testimony out of him?" Asks Tibbs.

"He's got to leave this out or we are…"

THE N Y CONNIVERS SERIES

18

Meanwhile, over at the defense's office, Brad Smith is in an animated pow-wow with counsel. While court official escorts lay in wait oblivious to their convo. "I want to testify and so does Tessa!" Brad articulates. "You've got to be kidding me!"
Yells Taliaferro.

THE N Y CONNIVERS SERIES

"Why not? I need to clear my name. Brad states with Tessa nodding in the affirmative.
"Putting you on the stand will certainly not only work against us but could possibly land you in that hot chair. Fried out of your mind."
Affirms Taliaferro.
"Why?"
Asks Brad.
"You are inundated with motives. Those jurors look like staved wolves from the Five Boroughs." Says Calista Cochran the other member on the defense team.
"You are buried way too deep in the circumstantial!" She continues.
"Your alibi could be instantly torn to shreds. Not a chance!"
Says Taliaferro.
Brad appears not buying in and the defense senses his stance as he looks across at Tessa.
"Put yourself in the mirror trying to answer these questions. Where were you when this murder went down? Why were you in NYC – vacationing? Why on that particular night? Why in that same state where your wife resides? You could have picked Hawaii or Jamaica for Christ's sake. Did you not move to Miami from NYC a few months prior? What were you and your new-found lover doing in NYC

on that weekend? They can insinuate it was to orchestrate or participate in your wife's rub-out? And on and on and on. And the beat goes on. Are you ready for such lines of questioning? Brad Smith, based on my two decades of experiences as a criminal defense attorney, I don't think you are ready for all this."

Says Taliaferro.

Neither Brad nor Tessa is sold on this apparent denial for them to take the witness stand. Taliaferro gets up from his chair and eyes his client.

"Brad, if you push it, we might just have to withdraw as your counsel."

"Will I get my money back? All of it?"

Asks Brad.

Taliaferro responds:

"We'll happily refund you a portion of the retainer." As the defense departed their office: Bang! Bang! Two shots rang out. With Samuel Taliaferro in the driver's seat and Calista Cochran in the front passenger seat the two rear tires deflated as a result of those rounds, the car flipped over. A gunman fled the scene in a Mercedes Benz. Moments later, a fire truck pulled up on the scene, followed by multiple NYPD vehicles. Ironically, two of those police officers included Detective Jonathan Hobbs and Jamie Johnson.

THE N Y CONNIVERS SERIES

Fortunately, the two attorneys walked away from the car wreck, unscathed.

THE N Y CONNIVERS SERIES

19

Rumor had it: Brad Smith, before his wife's death was working on securing millions of dollars to fund a Miami real estate deal. As the trial reconvened, his Realtor was called to testify. This surprise witness testified Smith had met with him multiple times regarding purchasing a piece of South Beach real estate.

THE N Y CONNIVERS SERIES

Next, Noel Pendergrass was called to the witness stand. The prosecution had the first crack at their witness.
"Mr. Pendergrass, what is your marital status?"
Asks Claudia Mendez.
"Married."
"Happily, or unhappily?"
"Move to strike!"
Shouts Taliaferro.
"Sidebar!"
Says Judge Thomas.
"Counsel, where are you taking this?
Asks the Judge.
"To the altar."
Says Taliaferro sarcastically.
"Just trying to prove my client enjoys awesome family life and does not engage in infidelity."
Says Claudia Mendez.
"You may continue your questioning, but you may want to avoid that track you are railing on."
States the Judge.
There wasn't much else for the Prosecution to squeeze out of the witness Noel Pendergrass. However, in regard to the tip, Pendergrass stated Brad had texted him and advised him he would be in NYC that weekend. Brad indicated he would be staying at the Airport Hampton. Additionally, he

THE N Y CONNIVERS SERIES

and Tessa would join him for a drink. That Pub meeting never occurred. Pendergrass pulled out his iPhone and that text was placed into evidence. When asked if he called Brad to find out why he no showed. Pendergrass said Brad Smith was the kind of man who had problems keeping an appointment during their tenure at the firm.

"Brad didn't show up,"

Pendergrass stated, and after watching the Breaking News about Beverly Smith's murder he sensed Brad could have possibly been involved.

THE N Y CONNIVERS SERIES

20

It was Taliaferro's turn to cross-examine Noel Pendergrass.
"Mr. Pendergrass, you have worked at least 3 years at the same firm with my client Brad Smith. Is that correct?"
"That is correct."
Says Noel Pendergrass.

THE N Y CONNIVERS SERIES

"Do you have a bias, prejudice, or triangular beef with Brad Smith.
"No. Why should I?"
Responds Pendergrass.
"Did you ever feel threatened by Brad Smith?" Asks Taliaferro.
"No."
"You were released from that firm. Weren't you?"
"Yes."
"What was the reason for your termination?"
"Objection!"
Says Claudia Mendez.
"Objection overruled."
Says Judge Thomas.
"Did your termination from the firm where you worked with Brad Smith make you determined to testify in this case?"
"No."
"Were you there when Beverly Smith was shot?" Asks Taliaferro.
"No."
"So, you have no evidence Brad Smith and Tessa Santos were the murderers?"
"No."
"Yet, you informed the detectives on the scene concerning Brad Smith's whereabouts?"
"I have no evidence."

THE N Y CONNIVERS SERIES

"Is it your testimony before this jury… You have no evidence that Brad Smith or Tessa Santos murdered Beverly Tyson-Smith?"
"It is."
"Did you meet with the prosecution to discuss your testimony?"
"Objection!"
Shouts the District Attorney – Claudia Mendez.
"Sustained!"
Retorts the Judge.
"Did you?' "No. No such thing."
Says Pendergrass.
"Are you indebted to the prosecution in any way?"
"No. I'm not."
"Are you still of the opinion Brad Smith had something to do with the murder of his wife Beverly Smith?" "Yes."
Responds Pendergrass.
"Why so?"
"I believe he had to motives to do so. When we worked together, he would always complain Beverly was putting pressure on him. He always felt I might disclose such statements. A week later, I got terminated from the firm. Plus, canceling his appointment with me and not letting me know, clearly states he was more than preoccupied on that NYC trip."

THE N Y CONNIVERS SERIES

Says Pendergrass.
"Are you a lawyer or do you specialize in the art of advocacy?"
Asks Taliaferro.
"No. I'm not."
"Were you ever in a love triangle relationship involving Brad Smith?"
"What are you talking about? Never did." Says Noel Pendergrass.
Taliaferro states and continues.
"Is anybody paying you to testify?"
"No. Not at all."
Noel Pendergrass responds. Your honor, I have no further questions."

THE N Y CONNIVERS SERIES

21

Michael Perez, Brad's Boss was next to take the witness stand. Perez testified: There was some chatter at the office relating to Brad and Beverly Smith. When asked about the reason to terminate Noel Pendergrass and if the gossip played a role in his decision to let Pendergrass go. Michael Perez said:

"No." Not wanting to go into his internal affairs at the firm, Michael Perez told Taliaferro several negligent complaints from clients against Pendergrass' and played a role in his dismissal from the firm. It had absolutely nothing to do with Brad or Beverly Tyson-Smith. In questioning the witness, the prosecution asked if knowing what he knows now if he would consider rehiring Pendergrass. Michael Perez said: "The firm has no desire to terminate its employees. However, when that glass is full, the next factor is the overflow. In other words, whenever cancer forms the best remedy is to cut it out before it spreads any further, contaminating the whole body." Taliaferro asked him if he saw Noel Pendergrass as cancer.

He dodged by responding:

"With Noel's skillset, he would be an asset to Wall Street or any relative financial sector. It was quite clear the prosecution on their questioning of their star witness Noel Pendergrass were trying to categorize him as someone without blemish, someone who would stand up for propriety. They were looking for anyone in the trial to back him up as a good, decent moral citizen. One who just wanted to help them solve this case.

THE N Y CONNIVERS SERIES

THE NEXT WITNESS IN THE TRIAL was Devon Scott, the Smith's personal Banker. Devon worked at the neighborhood bank which served the couple. Scott had to come clean as a whistle because all of Beverly Tyson – Smith's financial records were subpoenaed. Documents included: Insurance policies. Bank records. Bank monthly statements. As well as other assets. When questioned about Beverly's plan to visit the bank on the day after she was murdered. Devon Scott provided a photocopy of his calendar to the prosecution. This was subsequently shared with the defense team. He was also asked by both the Defense and the prosecution if he committed the murder of Beverly Tyson – Smith or knew anyone else who did. Devon Scott responded in the negative.

THE N Y CONNIVERS SERIES

22

Late in the trial, there were new developments. The prosecution elected to subpoena call records. Seemingly, they were prepared to like drowning prosecutors catch at a straw. Their evidence as described in the media did not sail. The phone records showed who called, at that time...whose phone talked to whom. Even so, not

THE N Y CONNIVERS SERIES

revealing what they had communicated. New evidence revealed Beverly Tyson – Smith placed a call to Tessa upon her arrival in Miami. Tessa did not take the call. Based on the timeline that call came in as a private call to Tessa Santos while she entered the mall, where she alleged later, Beverly stalked her.

Hours later, another call from Beverly's phone to Brad from her phone as a private number.

Meanwhile, on the day Beverly was murdered she did speak with Brad for half an hour. She was dead and Brad eventually declined to testify. Beverly also spoke with Noel Pendergrass for twelve minutes on the phone that evening before she was murdered. However, Pendergrass was never recalled testifying in the case.

THERE WAS ALSO testimony from the Coroner who performed the autopsy.

He stated there were three bullets retrieved from the head of Beverly Tyson – Smith. Meanwhile, the ballistics expert provided a statement that the bullets came from a 45 semi-automatic weapon.

Additionally, three bullets remained inside the magazine of that weapon. According to the Coroner's findings: The victim was shot at 8:35 pm on April 13, she died at approximately 8:47 pm – twelve minutes later. There were no other inflicted

wounds found on her body except for a neck fracture. The prosecution pressed for information relating to a potential struggle facilitated by the necktie.
"Yes. There were markings around her neck, and they were diametrical in the size of the necktie."
Said the Coroner. When the Defense cross-examined, Taliaferro asked:
"How severe were these impressions left by the necktie?"
The Coroner said,
"They were minimal."
"Were those impressions a result of a possible aggressive struggle or close to someone tying a knot speedily?"
Asked Taliaferro. "Additionally, the neck fracture was very telling of a potential struggle."
"It could have been in-between."
Said the Coroner.
"Why so?"
Asked Taliaferro.
"Because her neck was scarcely bruised. There were no concussions just minute bruises and a neck-fracture." States the Coroner.
"Did you have anything to do with the murder or knew of anyone who might have been involved?"
"No Sir." Replied the Coroner.

"Were you paid to provide this testimony to these jurors?"

"No. I was not paid to do this. It's based on my reconnaissance."

"Were you promised anything in return for your testimony?"

Asked Taliaferro.

The Coroner answered in a negative.

THE N Y CONNIVERS SERIES

23

As a character witness, the prosecution called Mr. Matthews, principal at Stuyvesant High School. He testified: "Brad and Bev were model students. They always got straight A's. They were adored by both the staff and faculty alike."

Some members of our staff epitomized them so much, they fashioned their relationship in that vein.

THE N Y CONNIVERS SERIES

He went on to recount their wedding where he toasted the bride and groom.

"I delivered their toast with pride. There were over 50 students from Stuyvesant High, along with their dates."

Upon cross-examination, Taliaferro asked:

"Did you ever in your wildest imagination envision, either of them trying to rub out each other?"

"Nothing is impossible, but they were so well glued together. I couldn't imagine the world ever severing that unique bond?"

Says Matthews.

Taliaferro continued,

"I want you to take a look at the defendant Brad Smith who is faced with the death penalty if found guilty. And talk to him like you did when you gave that toast at their wedding."

"Brad, the Bees come from heaven and so do the flowers. The bees are designed to subtract nectar from flowers to feed their young and provide sweetener for millions of people. Although I find it hard to believe you've done what is alleged. We at Stuyvesant high are all better because you and Bev were the two Bees." Several jurors engaged the edge of their seats. Meantime, the prosecution expressed uneasiness. "Thank you, Mr. Matthews, for your

THE N Y CONNIVERS SERIES

testimony. Your honor, I have no further questions for this witness. Says Taliaferro.

THE N Y CONNIVERS SERIES

24

The Defense called Margaret Santos, Tessa's mother to testify. Tessa's Mom claimed Tessa was a straight-A student, who stayed almost to herself. Additionally, when Tessa's peers engaged in partying, she would stay at home and curl up with her school textbooks. She didn't want to have much to do with the toxic crowds.

"Do you know if Tessa had anything to do with this murder?" Asked the defense.

THE N Y CONNIVERS SERIES

Margaret Santos said:
"I don't believe Tessa was involved."
"Do you believe Tessa would encourage anyone to commit such an act?"
"If she knew of someone planning to commit such an act, she would ultimately talk them out of it."
Said Margaret Santos.
The prosecution pressed her regarding Tessa's habit as a lover of alcohol.
Her Mom said:
"Her dad and I were never big drinkers. However, we always had some beer, wine, or champagne for guests when they came."
The prosecution also asked if Tessa frequented the shooting range. Her mom in Tessa's defense claimed "Tessa was always afraid of guns. At home when they watched a movie, which was a shoot them up Bang! Bang! Tessa would amble to her room and dive into a good book."
"Have you ever been to South Beach, Miami?"
Asked Claudia Mendez. "No. I've never been to South Beach, but I've read about it and seen movie footage depicting that community."
Says Margaret Santos. "You seem to paint your daughter as a saint."

THE N Y CONNIVERS SERIES

To which Taliaferro objected. Judge Thomas overruled it. "Would someone with those character traits wander around at South Beach?"
Asks Claudia Mendez.
"It depends.
" Says Margaret Santos.
"The Pastor of our church may have never visited South Beach, but I could imagine he has some version of that scenery in his house or else he would not give his wife nine kids."
She continued.
The courtroom erupts with laughter. Claudia Mendez seemed to have lost her footing. Judge Thomas scans the courtroom.
"Counsel Mendez?"
"Your honor, the prosecution rests."
"Mr. Taliaferro?"
"Your honor the Defense rests."
"Are you ready for your closing statements?"
Asks Judge Claude Thomas. Mendez graces the lectern. Before saying one word she takes in the jury. You can hear a pin drop.
She catches most attendees in the room waiting for the next shoe to drop.

THE N Y CONNIVERS SERIES

25

Brad Smith and Tessa Santos, both defendants fix their eyes and body language in support of their defense Samuel Taliaferro. He argues: "It's human nature to punish the perpetrator in any murder case. Hang them high, place them on skid row, electrocute them. It's ingrained in us to seek justice in any such brutal ordeal. Our prisons are saturated with

THE N Y CONNIVERS SERIES

the male species: most of them for crimes they didn't commit.

In this case. In this case, evidence is certainly lacking against my clients. Even though the prosecution is on a quest to find the whodunit. There is a lack of evidence linking Brad Smith to that murder. My client is the husband, and the beneficiary is irrelevant.

As per the law, we need to find guilt beyond any reasonable doubt. However, let me restate: There has been no physical evidence presented that connects our clients: Brad Smith or Tessa Santos to this murder. Not one shred of evidence.

In this age of high-tech surveillance and forensics. You must find something, any spec of DNA. Not just fingerprints on previously delivered documents and a necktie previously worn by the defendant Mr. Brad Smith, her husband, who as of recently lived with her in that same house."

Like a vacuum, Taliaferro sucks in the entire jury. He continues:

"I see in this case bias. I see prejudice. I see a fermented love triangle.

Bias because he's a man. Prejudice because he's an accomplished businessman, an adept stockbroker. Immersed in a fermented love triangle barreled by Noel Pendergrass because he passed him up on a

relocation assignment vacancy which landed the defendant in Miami.

Subsequently, Pendergrass was terminated and sought revenge by forcibly installing himself in their relationship, thus creating an unwarranted love triangle. There's insufficient evidence linking the defendants to the murder of Beverly Tyson–Smith.

To formulate a guilty verdict, in this case, you must beyond any doubt find substantial evidence. There is a lack thereof. So, you must acquit. In closing, we should never lower our standards of justice to fit the paucity of evidence."

Taliaferro returns to his seat in high spirits.

THE N Y CONNIVERS SERIES

26

Claudia Mendez steps up for the prosecution. She gets right down to business: "I don't celebrate the death penalty…I believe all of us were beautifully and wonderfully made. Even so, we are faced with a task. One which demands justice. It does not matter if we parade character witness after character witness who in solidarity lend their

support to the defendants. What matters is that as upholders of the law, we do our jobs and do it well. I feel it is necessary when a man's love for his wife turns to hate and then he brutally murders her he should be reprimanded.

That same man who gave you the first kiss, maybe your first orgasm, planted the first hickey on your neck. Telling you what he wouldn't do to protect you. Mentioned sweet nothings in your ears, brought you flowers and other gifts when you didn't even anticipate receiving them. Wined and dined you. Massaged your neck. Held your hands as you crossed the street together.

Then he meets some pretty babe with her curves protruding as muscles. Premeditatedly, he flips and "Bang! Bang! Bang!" He shoots you in the head. Knowingly, he's the only beneficiary. Nursing plans to exploit your assets on his new lady and cherished real estate. He deserves the death penalty.

The defense spoke about bias, prejudice, and a fermented love triangle. There is no bias. There is no prejudice, there is no fermented love triangle. Brad Smith was struggling; he was busted after asking for a divorce from his wife. Karma? Call it what you will. If the cap fits. Let him wear it."

Brad tears up.

THE N Y CONNIVERS SERIES

"There were millions of dollars at stake with him being the sole beneficiary. There were no evidentiary ties linking his ex-coworker Noel Pendergrass to his estranged wife.

We've subpoenaed her phone log and even though it registered one call made to her on the day she was murdered. No one claimed they ever saw both of them together except on that night when both of you got so drunk and he volunteered to drive you home. Detectives Jonathan Hobbs and Jamie Johnson testified, and I paraphrase: When they showed up at the Hotel where Brad Smith overnighted along with his female companion Tessa Santos on the night of the murder: They found the two defendants hastily packing to catch a flight back to Miami.

There is only one person who had motives to and or to delegate the murder of his wife Beverly Tyson–Smith. That individual is the defendant - her husband Brad Smith aided by his accomplice and a new lover -Tessa Santos As jurors, it's your obligation to find them guilty as charged. " Prosecutor Claudia Mendez said, gave the jury a challenging stare and returned to her seat."

THE N Y CONNIVERS SERIES

27

Judge Thomas gaveled, and after some brief remarks, he summoned the jurors to deliberate. Their mandate: a unanimous verdict of guilty or not guilty.

Inside this unorthodox underground jury room, a large conference table accommodates twelve chairs, a clock on the wall, a water cooler, a coat rack, a dry-

erase whiteboard, a coffee maker, and three windows. Some jurors huddled around the table. While some still overwhelmed from the trial vented their agreements and disagreements in a separate second huddle at the door. The effervescent guard barges in and conducts an authentic headcount.
"All twelve accounted for."
She says and then leaves closing the door behind him. The Head Juror or Juror # 1 immediately takes charge and instructs the jurors in that second huddle to join the others who are already seated at the table. She then reshuffles her stacks of notes. While the latecomers are caught jockeying for position.
"The lowest number sits next to my left hand and number twelve will automatically end up next to my right. The sooner we can get this over with, the merrier."
Says the Head Juror.
Of course, being left-handed, she caters mostly to what's left of herself. A 32- year-old Lesbian and graduate of Yale Law School, she's pulling no punches. The jurors comply at her command. The HJ eyes the clock and proceeds:
"We are here today to deliberate a very unusual case…"
"That's a given!"

THE N Y CONNIVERS SERIES

Interjects juror # 2, that elderly Caucasian man – old enough to be the father of Beverly Tyson–Smith. The HJ continues:
"However, Judge Thomas commanded us to return a unanimous verdict. I sense a divide. Even so, let's deliver a win up or down for the sake of justice."
Juror # 2 is adamant.
"How are we going to do that?"
"We will endeavor to focus our debate on the evidence in this case. Hopefully, we've already tuned out all other outside influences."
Says HJ.
"That is a given. Even so, we are entitled to interject our opinions by drawing inferences from those situations."
Says Juror # 4 the man of color and ex-cop with the NYPD.
The HJ continues:
"You may. However, let's keep those inferences to a minimum. Else we could be stuck debating forever. As you already know. According to the evidence: this couple was madly in love, got married, and fell out of love. Now the weaker sex has been murdered."
"Don't contaminate the jury by telling us how to vote Madam HJ. Plus, I disagree with you, referring to this murdered woman as the weaker sex. There was

nothing puny about her. She was the one who purchased that weapon which took her life."

Says Juror # 7, that female African American woman with roots embedded in the advertising industry.

"What are you saying?"

Asks the HJ.

"According to the evidence: Beverly Tyson – smith owned the bulk of the assets in that relationship. Her worthless husband Brad Smith aka B.S. went to South Beach, Florida. Met a woman and squandered his money. Like the prodigal son, he returned home. Instead of coming clean based on his cheating A… he demanded a D."

"What's a D?"

Asks Juror # 10, that long-bearded Indian professor. "You sat in the box. "D" means divorce. Upon realizing his wife's full net worth, he asks for the exit and murders her; so, he can accommodate that gold-digger from Miami. Beverly Tyson Smith wasn't weak. She provided an inheritance just in case some kids came along. That's a strong woman. Much like Queen Esther."

"Your point is well taken." Says Juror # 8, the man from the construction business. "Yep. I agree with your scenario." Says HJ. "I disagree. They made that money together. The fact that they sat up a joint bank account gives reason to believe what hers was his

THE N Y CONNIVERS SERIES

and what's his was hers." Says the millennial Gay persona. "Can we focus
on the case and get a verdict?"
Asks the HJ.
Juror # 3 that elderly woman who served for 3 decades as a Librarian, has her hand up eager for her turn, and gets it.
"We are. It is necessary we explore and draw inferences from the situation as was stated by Juror # 2."
"It's necessary we expediently explore and draw references…"
Says HJ.
"What's the rush? This is not supposed to be a quickie."
Says Juror # 6, the Latino woman, and Train Conductor.
"It's not but we need to close soon. If we don't like the HJ said we could be on this till eternity. Let's put these two horses in the stable so we can get out of here."
Says Juror # 9, that Latino used car Salesman from Long Island. The HJ nods her head in the affirmative and moves to the whiteboard. She draws two columns: Guilty/Not Guilty.
"Agreed! Let's vote." and continues:
"Those for guilty raise your hands…"

THE N Y CONNIVERS SERIES

"Not so fast. I thought we all made up the jury. We've not heard anything from Jurors 11 and 12. Yet, what happened they weren't endowed with the gift of speech, or we are content with voting without hearing from them?"
Articulates Juror # 7.
"Brad Smith did not kill his wife. As the defense so eloquently stated: There's a paucity of evidence in this case. The only reason we are here deliberating is that this proceeding fits the legal format. It's all about the process.
We all know it's suicide. Beverly Tyson–Smith bought that gun from the neighborhood gun shop. She traveled to Miami on a bus in search of Brad Smith, so she could waste him. She didn't find him. So, she tracked down Tessa Santos his mistress, and stalked her, thinking she would lead her to Brad. Tessa made a detour en route. Realizing she had lost her only guide to Brad Smith her husband she returned home and shot herself. Bang! Bang! Bang!"
Says Juror # 12, that RN who believes she can fix everything. Juror # 11, that female hairstylist from Brooklyn is adamant.
"So, if that's factual. Who strangled Beverly Tyson-Smith? And why was his necktie roped inside her left hand?

THE N Y CONNIVERS SERIES

28

The Head Juror seems ready to push this deliberation into high gear. "Now that everyone has argued the case. I feel it appropriate to call for a vote."

Several jurors are not in sync with her decision. She displays reluctance to become involved in their Mickey Mouse game of chess.

She states authoritatively.

THE N Y CONNIVERS SERIES

"All those for a guilty vote that the defendant Brad Smith and Tessa Santos murdered Beverly Tyson-Smith, please raise your right hand."

"I thought this was about a verdict. This is not an oath. Why were we asked to raise our right hand? Come on!" States Juror # 4.

"Do you have a better idea?"

Asks the HJ.

"I suggest we all get up from our seats. Move to that whiteboard and write our vote thereon."

Says Juror # 12.

"I like that inkling. However, we are not here for theatrics or a spectacle. We were sent here according to the judge to return a unanimous verdict, guilty or not guilty. Not here to strut our stuff."

Says HJ. Sensing HJ going for her notes, Juror # 12 does likewise.

"According to my notes, and I have been writing since Judge Thomas gaveled in and gaveled out. And frankly, the defendants are guilty. They had every reason to commit that murder. There's no coincidence: Let's face it. Based on Noel Pendergrass's testimony, they traveled from Miami to New York City on that particular weekend. Lodged at a nearby hotel 15 minutes from the crime scene and 15 minutes from the airport. How convenient? Kill and Flee through airport security."

THE N Y CONNIVERS SERIES

Most of the jurors are listening carefully.
Juror # 12 continues.
"They strategically planned their attack as well as their getaway."
"Yes! If those two detectives were delayed by a few double-parked vehicles. The defendants could have boarded that flight back to Miami or even caught a direct flight to Havana, Cuba. Thereby remaining at large. Junior Castro would not release them even if America decided to pay more for their Cuban Cigars. The defendants are both guilty as charged."
Says HJ.
At this point, the HJ has sucked the air out of the room. She continues, riding this momentum as she correlates her notes.
"I was just drawing an inference. Not sure I'm ready to show my hand."
Says juror # 12. The HJ connects with Juror # 2.
"Juror # 2, what's your vote?"
She asks.
"I'm very agile at 75. Thanks. That whiteboard is only a few feet away. Again, I ask myself: Why did Brad Smith have to shoot his wife? Why did he?"
"He grew to hate her after he met Tessa Santos. She must have been a real test."
The Head Juror interjects. Juror # 2 continues.

THE N Y CONNIVERS SERIES

"A separation is not the end of the world. Life goes on. I was separated from my first wife. I did not murder her or myself - kill. Even though she walked away from that relationship with a stash. All that money I had stored under the bed mattress. I remarried a woman much younger than her. To me, she's more than my mistress."
"Is that why you stay so agile?"
Asks Juror # 11. Juror # 2 smiles and continues.
"It was then I decided if I ever go down that divorce route, everything has to be divided 50/50. Tessa Santos was an accomplice to this murder. She's as guilty as they come. Sorry, I'm not an advocate for ..."
Juror # 2 walks over to the board and next to his name writes guilty. The whiteboard reflects two jurors supportive of guilty verdicts: The Head Juror and Juror # 2.
"I thought it was very much agreed upon. I'll do the writing on the whiteboard." "
I finished school in the days of plat-formed shoes, bell-bottom-pants, and afro-picks.'
Says Juror # 2 as he takes his seat. Meanwhile, the HJ kept on digging for votes.

THE N Y CONNIVERS SERIES

29

Juror # 5 is caught not only doodling but deep in thought. "Where do you stand, Juror # 3 - guilty?" Juror # 3 still buried in her notes, comes up for air. "This is a complicated situation." She quibbles. " None of the evidence presented gives any credence to the defendants committing the murder. Anyone

can find himself or herself at the wrong place at the wrong time."

"What are you saying?"

Asks Juror # 4.

"Police officers on numerous occasions arrest innocent people simply because they are in the wrong place at the wrong time. This can easily happen if you are near a crime scene or match the description of a suspected criminal or even related to the victim. Especially if you are black and wearing a hoodie."

"Okay. Point well taken."

Says HJ.

"I'm not done... In a recent incident at a Florida Waffle House, two people were wrongfully arrested. After someone called the police claiming that they were trespassing and stealing.

When the police officer arrived, the couple was waiting for the customer service telephone number after being overcharged for a cold drink. The officer allegedly drew his Taser before arresting the couple. Luckily, those charges were dropped eventually.

Nevertheless, not all of those wrongfully arrested are as fortunate. If the police believe they have the right suspect, and evidence cannot prove otherwise, an innocent person can get incarcerated. Even if you can fight the charges, a wrongful arrest cannot only

damage your reputation but could place you in the electric chair if warranted…"
Interrupting is Juror # 8.
"How does that apply to this case?"
He asks.
"If I may? When your turn comes around, make sure you have notes to corroborate. Please hold your horses. In another incident: A Miami teen was wrongfully arrested and charged for a shooting he didn't commit. Consequently, video evidence showed the teen shopping with his mother at the time of the shooting, he, along with another suspect, was eventually released. However, because the incident made the local news, he faced social stigma from people in his community. There are mountains of scenarios depicting these kinds of arrests. We need to do our homework before reaching a verdict."
"Well stated! Ada boy!"
Says Juror # 3, as she heads to the water fountain.
The HJ waits for a commitment from Juror # 5.
Juror # 5 leaves through his catalog of notes and states: "I still need to review additional evidence."

THE N Y CONNIVERS SERIES

30

Juror # 3 eyes Juror # 12 across the table. Subsequently, Juror # 3 saunters to the coffee maker counter. She samples the brew and then draws a full cup.
Juror # 2 ambles over next to her.
"How's the coffee?"
Asks Juror # 12.

"Pretty good. There's nothing like a great cup of coffee when you need it."
Responds Juror # 3.
"Tough sleeping? Yeah?"
Asks Juror # 12 as she draws a full cup. She tastes.
"Not bad!"
"Where are you on the verdict? Those two defendants seem buried deep in it.?"
Asks juror # 3.
"They are? Submerged? Hook, line, and sinker."
Asks Juror # 12.
The other ten jurors are waiting around the conference table. The HJ tries hiding her impatience with the process.
"My intuition tells me they are complicit in these crimes."
Says Juror # 12.
"Complicit?"
Asks Juror # 3.
"Yes. Complicit."
"How?"
Asks Juror # 3 as if not knowing the meaning of the Comp word.
"Complicity is the act of helping or encouraging another individual to commit a crime. It is also commonly referred to as aiding and abetting. A complicit person is said to be an accomplice.

THE N Y CONNIVERS SERIES

Indeed, accomplices can also face the same penalties, including prison time. Both of them could wind up in the hot chair side by side."
Says the all-knowing she can fix everything – Juror # 12.
"Jurors, you can finish your debate over at the table. We've been waiting!"
Yells the Head Juror
"Yes. Let's close this deal."
Says Juror # 8.
"So, they are hitched together as he was with his wife Beverly?"
Says Juror # 12 as she continues her verbiage with Juror # 3.
"Yep. I wish everyone would hurry up and vote. So, we can get out of here before midnight. I hate having to wake my husband up. He prefers waking me up."
Juror # 3 says. They begin walking towards the table.
"Midnight? We would be fortunate if this deliberation wraps within 24 hours. So tonight, might be your raincheck."
Responds Juror # 12.
"People are so frustrated it's beginning to feel like that House of debate. Most are fed up with the process." The HJ overhears and advises.
"Please leave your politics at the coffee table."
"That would be a miracle."

THE N Y CONNIVERS SERIES

Says Juror # 12 as they both take their seats across from each other at the table.

THE N Y CONNIVERS SERIES

31

Dirty looks from the other jurors beam towards jurors 3 and 12.
"Where are we with the voting?" Asks Juror # 3.
"So far only two votes still. Both in favor of guilty." Says Juror # 10.
"Judge Thomas reminded us to use common sense in our deliberations."

THE N Y CONNIVERS SERIES

Says Juror 12. The Head Juror sensing that Juror # 12 is attempting to helm the debate, asks:
"What are you saying Juror # 12."
"I'm saying: We're faced with a lack of evidence against the defendants. While it remains a fact that the victim was murdered. Common sense tells us the defendants were not at the scene at the time of the murder."
"Where were they?"
Asks Juror # 4. He continues…
"During my career as a law enforcement officer. I have never heard of someone shooting another without being present."
"I think you should give me a chance to finish what I'm saying."
Says Juror # 12.
"You have said enough. Plus, you wasted our time; you and your Sistren at the coffee maker… with all that bedroom talk."
"Let's get back to the debate at hand! Let her finish." Says HJ.
Juror # 4 rudely gets up from the table and ambles over to the coffee station.
"Once a cop always a cop! He must be a happy one." Yells juror # 12.
"That's right. I'll always uphold the law. Happy or sad."

THE N Y CONNIVERS SERIES

Yells juror # 4.
"So, let us get back to where I was before I was rudely interrupted. It is clear the defendants were not the actual killers."
Says Juror # 12.
Juror # 4 returns to the table spilling some of his hot coffee on himself.
"So why were they hurrying to flee New York City where the murder occurred?"
Asks Juror # 4.
"Documentary evidence showed they were booked on a returned flight to Miami early that morning. Pronto…"
States Juror # 7.
"That was their alibi. I wished they produced a better one. That murder was not only premeditated, but they also tried to get away. It's obvious: The only reason they came to NYC was to commit that murder."
Says Juror # 4.
"So, that means you support a guilty verdict, Juror # 4?"
Asks the HJ.
"That's not what I am saying."
Responds Juror # 4, promptly.
"It's fair to say that's what you're insinuating?" Asks the HJ.

THE N Y CONNIVERS SERIES

"Please do not put words in my mouth. I'm here to uphold the law…"
"Really? Really? Really?"
Interrupts Juror # 7.
"Yes. Uphold? I shall."
Responds Juror # 4.
Several jurors erupt with sarcastic laughter.
"The only fingerprints lifted of the defendants were from a previously worn necktie by Brad Smith and on the divorce documents which were overseen by Tessa Santos."
Says Juror # 12.
"Okay. So, you are saying: Those redactions found in those divorce documents were made by the defendant, Tessa Santos?"
Asks Juror # 4.
"Now you are trying to instill evidence… I mean words in my mouth."
Responds Juror # 12.
 "We're not here to retry this case. We're here to produce unanimity."
Says HJ.
"I predict this is all going to end up as a hung jury."
Says Juror # 2.
"Juror # 12 what's your vote?"
Asks the HJ.
Juror # 12 responds, "

THE N Y CONNIVERS SERIES

At this point, we need to uncover all the facts! How does one manufacture something out of something? How do you find evidence when there is no, there, there? Only God can do such a thing."

THE N Y CONNIVERS SERIES

32

At this point, the Head Juror announces a recess. The Guard shows up and exercises the door. In the meantime, a line of jurors approaches the coffee station. The headliners include jurors # 9, 5, 11 and 6. Juror # 5 quickly fills his cup. Juror # 5, before filling his cup states:

THE N Y CONNIVERS SERIES

"I'm bothered not only by the vast lack of evidence in this case but by this entire process."

"That's a shared feeling but you have a line of jurors behind you. They are waiting to get a cup of coffee too. So, please do not hold up the line."

States Juror # 9.

"I'm very glad that another jury feels the way I feel regarding the entire trial and deliberation. If this continues, we can certainly reach unanimity. Why did we have to do this on a Friday night?"

Says Juror # 5.

"Remember, common sense, as our fellow juror said: is a prerequisite toward unanimity."

Says Juror # 9.

Juror # 5 finally gets out of the way to facilitate Juror # 11's approach to the coffee station.

Juror # 12 joins the line and states:

"Make sure you save me some of that robust coffee."

"I thought you were already maxed out on coffee."

Says Juror # 5.

"No. I'm not. Just a die-hard coffee lover. So much you can call me Coffee Bean."

Responds Juror # 12.

"I wished you would stop talking in parables. You even did so at times during our deliberation."

Says Juror # 5 as Juror # 6 fills his cup.

Juror # 6 tastes and reacts to the hot brew.

THE N Y CONNIVERS SERIES

Juror # 12 continues,
"I once heard a story about a carrot, an egg, and a coffee bean."
"You?"
Asks Juror # 11.
"Got it! They took each other to court and the egg won because it came before the chicken. Then the chicken devoured the coffee bean thinking it was a corn kernel."
Interjects Juror # 5.
"Far from it." Says Juror # 12, now with multiple deliberating eyes focused on her. "When the carrot was placed in the boiling water it became soft. When the egg was placed in the boiling water it became hard. However, when the coffee bean was placed in the boiling water, it changed the color of the water…"
"That's the reason you signed up to do this?"
Interrupts Juror # 11.
"We are back in session!"
Yells the Head Juror.
The jurors return to their seats discombobulated.

THE N Y CONNIVERS SERIES

33

Juror # 2 remains standing as if his seat is on fire. He gains everyone's attention before uttering a single word.
"According to the autopsy results: Beverly Tyson – Smith suffered a mild neck fracture. Looking at the evidence, we need to drill down on this one. Did she

try to hang herself with that necktie inside her bathroom? When that failed, did she fetch her gun and rush to her living room, smash the glass on the door, leave that door ajar, and then shoot herself in the head while holding on to that necktie with her non-shooting hand?
Then cried, Romeo! Romeo! Romeo!"
States Juror # 2.
"There's nothing in the autopsy report which states Beverly Tyson–Smith was intoxicated or drugged. Why would anyone go through such a routine to kill themselves? Crimes are not done that way. Your debate is half-baked."
Says Juror # 4.
"Aah! So, you are saying: Beverly Tyson–Smith committed a crime?"
Asks Juror # 2.
"No. I'm not."
Says Juror # 4.
"Well then? What are you advocating?"
Juror # 2 asks. Juror # 4 is mute at this point. He stutters. Juror # 2 seizes the moment.
"You are saying if I heard you correctly. You are saying based on your law enforcement experience the victim committed suicide? I advocate that she did and left us to believe she was murdered by her husband and his girlfriend because they visited NYC

that weekend. Miss head Juror, I've changed my vote to not guilty. Let's not fool ourselves. Nor waste our time when we could be in our beds getting a good night's sleep."

"Are you tired? Do you want to sleep? Pops, what you just said and did does not move the needle toward a guilty vote. I can't believe at your age you cannot keep your word. You are the one who's wasting our time. This is Friday night. If as jurors we don't produce something substantial we could be here until Monday."

Says Juror # 4.

"I'm not your Papa."

The other jurors are taken aback as these two duke it out verbally.

"If I were, I would not have dropped you on your head on the wet pavement."

Continues Juror # 2.

"He has the right to change his vote if he wishes. Meanwhile, let's refrain from calling each other names or attacking our fellow jurors. I realize for us this is a tough assignment. However, we all signed up for this…remember?"

Says the Head Juror as Juror # 4 interrupts her.

"This is unbelievable. Are you getting ready to flip? That would be a terrible decision as leader of the group…"

THE N Y CONNIVERS SERIES

"Are you going to cite her? I don't get it. Why do we keep fighting instead of voting our conscience based on the evidence?"
States Juror # 7.
"Head Juror, I vote guilty. They are both guilty. That's my conscientious decision."
Jurors are stunned as Juror # 4 dropped that bomb. He continues:
"Now we are back to where the votes were before the recess."
The HJ updates the stats on the whiteboard.
"Good riddance! That will keep you quiet."
Says Juror # 12 as she stares down Juror # 4.
The HJ interjects:
"Who else wishes to cast their vote?"
Juror # 4 gets up and walks toward the coffee station and taps up his cup.

THE N Y CONNIVERS SERIES

34

Returning to his seat, Juror # 4 puts his coffee on the table and scans the faces of his fellow jurors.

"I've been deeply puzzled all the while as to how these two people could be complicit in the murder of Beverly Tyson – Smith."

"They did not. That is a figment of some people's imagination!"

THE N Y CONNIVERS SERIES

Shouts Juror # 12.

Juror # 5 ignores the rhetoric and continues:

Although we don't know who pulled the trigger of that 45 semi-automatic gun recovered at the crime scene. There are multiple occurrences of complicity in a murder. Let's say Tessa held the gun with her fingerprints concealed. Brad said, 'Shoot her, shoot Beverly," and Bang! Bang! Bang! Beverly is shot in the head. Brad and Tessa functioned as an enterprise in Beverly's murder."

"What if it was vice versa?"

Asks Juror # 4.

"Same difference. Most of us are too young to remember Derek Bentley, who was convicted of murder after his accomplice in a burglary, Christopher Craig, shot a police officer. 'Let him have it, Chris' Bentley said. Perhaps telling Craig to hand over his weapon. – or perhaps as the prosecution argued, urging him to fire.

Under the term 'joint enterprise' Derek Bentley had provided what is known as 'assistance or encouragement' and was therefore just as guilty as Christopher Craig, the principal offender. Derek Bentley was ultimately hanged for a shooting in which he didn't hold the gun."

States Juror # 5.

"That happened back in 1952, didn't it?"

THE N Y CONNIVERS SERIES

Asks the HJ.

"A more controversial example was the conviction of Lenox Mitchell and her boyfriend Michael Hall. One night in 2007, the couple and two other people they were with, got into a fight in a car parked outside a Bradford pub, with a man named Andrew Ayers, over who booked the taxi. Mitchell and Hall then left the scene so that she could search a different part of the park (like Cinderella) for her lost shoes. In the meantime, the other two defendants went to a nearby house and armed themselves with knuckledusters and other weapons. In a second, a more serious fight ensued, which did not involve Mitchell or Hall, Ayres was killed. The two armed men were convicted of murder, but so too were Mitchell and Hall. Their convictions were upheld by an appeals court in October 2016."

Juror # 5 has the attention of the other eleven jurors. So, he rambles on.

"In another case often cited by campaigners against the abuse of joint enterprise, Jordan Cunliffe, who was then 15, was one of three people convicted of the 2007 murder of Garry Newlove. Newlove was killed by a kick to the neck by one of a group of local teenagers, who attacked him after he accused them of vandalizing his car. Cunliffe argues that although he was present, he never touched Newlove – a claim

THE N Y CONNIVERS SERIES

supported by the fact that he suffers from a degenerative eye condition and was registered as blind at the time.

If you can do that to a blind 15-year-old, you can do it to anyone –and it's been done to a lot of people, his mother, Janet, said to the Guardian two years ago. Cunliffe remains in prison. That's the way the mop flops and the cookie crumbles in our judicial system."

"You have put a lot of food on our plate. How do you vote?"

Asks the HJ.

"On that premise of the joint enterprise. I vote guilty. The two defendants are guilty as charged."

Says Juror # 5.

The Head Juror sprints to the whiteboard and adds another guilty vote to the stats.

THE N Y CONNIVERS SERIES

35

The tabulated votes on the whiteboard now read Jurors #'s 4. 5, 6 & HJ = Guilty. Juror # 2 = Not Guilty. The HJ sensing momentum in the voting process becomes embolden. Focused now more than ever she asks:
"Juror # 7, where do you stand in the voting process? Are you yea or nay?"

THE N Y CONNIVERS SERIES

"Evidence is evidence. There's a preponderance of evidence that supports suicide. Beverly Tyson – Smith beyond the shadow of a doubt, found herself in the category of battered women. Photographic evidence presented in court showed her riding one horse to the trail and the other horse following in tow led by a rope. What woman in her right state of mind would indulge in such a feat? She felt no one wanted her and that she had lost it all."

"No. She didn't."

Says Juror # 8.

"According to an article on Mental Health which was Op-ed in DAME, titled: WHY ARE MORE WOMEN COMMITTING SUICIDE? The author states: *Every day for nearly six months after Natalie* turned 45, she thought about taking the turn on her way to work so sharply that she would overshoot the road, go airborne, and land in the river. She imagined it all happening quickly: the sensation of flying, the huge splash as the car hit the water, and then the water surrounding her, as the car descended to the river bottom. Natalie imagined herself not holding her breath, not panicking, not trying to escape as the car filled with water, but rather breathing the same as if she were above the water. She imagined the air in her lungs being displaced with water and then losing consciousness. A Catholic, Natalie imagined herself saying an Act of Contrition and praying for forgiveness,*

THE N Y CONNIVERS SERIES

but mostly she imagined a peaceful death. **Simone***, 57, had been taking anti-anxiety medication for nearly two years for stress before she got into a hot bath with a half-full bottle of pills, a bottle of wine, and a razor blade. **Chloe***, 22, wasn't even sure what she was doing when she knotted the scarves together, tied them to the bars of the headboard of her bed, lay down, and then slipped the noose around her neck. She'd read that hanging was the easiest and least painful method of suicide and she was ready to die.

"Although suicide tendencies are more common in men. Women are now aggressively competing in those stats."
States Juror # 7.
"The author of that Op-ed has not seen the evidence in this case. When it comes to Beverly Tyson Smith, I disagree. It was less than a week before her death that she won over a million dollars at Belmont. How dare you assume she had lost it all and found herself in the category of losers?"
Asks Juror # 8.
'It's a given, that when most women lose the man they deeply loved to another woman, no matter what comes their way materially, they still feel like a loser. It takes work and time to heal from those bastards. The things they put us through. It is no longer known

as heartbreak. We can call it Soul-break. It happened to me.
Yes. She felt she had lost it all, money could not fill that void."
Says Juror # 10.
"If I may continue," says Juror # 7 who is still on her feet and wouldn't let up.
"If a woman wants to fake a crime, there's nothing to stand in her way. Someone mentioned in this trial: A woman is classified as the weaker sex. That is total baloney. A woman is built to bring children into the world."
"Preach my Sistren!"
Says Juror # 12.
"I have two kids of my own through natural childbirth. It's a darn painful process to give birth that way. Plus going through morning sickness and a child instantly and constantly kicking you in the gut for months on end before your water breaks."
"Yep."
Says Juror # 12.
"That power is given to us. So, don't tell me faking a murder such as this is unimaginable and unsubstantiated. So, don't tell me such a thing was hard for Beverly Tyson–Smith to orchestrate."
States Juror # 7 as she breaks down in tears and draws sympathetic attention.

THE N Y CONNIVERS SERIES

"With all that said and all that pain a woman goes through, you are considering a guilty verdict. Yes?" Asks the HJ.
"Do you know what you are putting me through? If I make such a decision now and before this process ends there's something that I hadn't thought of, then I'm either stuck or have to flip like a rat. I can't tarnish my reputation like that."
Says Juror # 7.
"I thought you came to the deliberation prepared…"
Says the HJ.
"Did you?"
Asks Juror # 7 regaining her presence of mind.
"I did."
Responds the HJ.
"That's why there are so many innocent people in jail. As our leader, you came prepared. I thought this process was a deliberating event to find the truth based on evidence and common sense.
We take a little here and a little there and with the evidence gleaned from the trial we produce a verdict. What you just stated indicates you are willing to sabotage this process."
"I agree."
Says Juror # 12.
"No wonder you've got to dig so hard to produce votes. This should be an easy process if you let the

proceedings work itself out… Instead, you have forced your decision on the process and want others to tag along. You are bordering on Jury contamination. Watch your step Ms."

"The HJ darts towards Juror # 7 and is restrained by Juror # 4.

"This process stinks! The defendants are not guilty as charged."

Says juror # 7.

"I'm sorry you feel that way about the process. Your vote is accounted for. Now we are 4 guilty and 2 not guilty."

Says HJ as she etches the stats on the whiteboard.

THE N Y CONNIVERS SERIES

36

Juror # 9 has been standing for some time now and inching to interject deliberately.

"I hate this process. I can't believe I took time away from my 9-9 for this. It's like trying to get a client to purchase a lemon he doesn't want to drive home. You toy with their emotions. Paint a picture of a cross country trip. Then you sell them the car you want them

THE N Y CONNIVERS SERIES

to purchase and not the car they want to own. Then he takes it home with buyer's remorse. He's not happy with his purchase because it wasn't him but you who decided for him. Is it possible Head Juror, that you are doing what you can to peel off guilty votes? Are you attempting to rig the process?"

"I beg to differ. How dare you accuse me of selling a lemon? If that's what you do for a living, please don't cast your shadows on others."

Says HJ.

"Have it your way. Anyway, I am not going to strike my talking points. Please don't take us down that rabbit hole."

HJ is furious over those remarks.

"Come on. There's no reason to get into a fight over the procedure. We're here to produce a verdict and you Miss Head Juror to deliver it to Judge Claude Thomas by Saturday morning. Good thing he's not Jewish." Says Juror # 9.

The HJ asks:

"Juror # 9, what's your vote?"

"To be honest. As far as I see it, using common sense and weighing the evidence...Brad Smith, after deciding to abort the marriage with his wife Beverly Tyson-Smith, became penniless. Based on the testimony from his realtor, Smith explored the options of purchasing a million-dollar piece of real

estate in Miami–South Beach. Knowing he had no money to do so and no funders in the cue. He was relying on the cash out from his wife's insurance policy and other beneficiary assets.

Brad Smith planned the murder and brought his girlfriend Tessa Santos into it as an accomplice. If Smith for any reason gets acquitted, he would no doubt use the money he stands to inherit and close on that property in South Beach from his murdered wife's assets. We must stop him.

Therefore, I cast my vote in the guilty column. Both defendants are complicit in the murder of Beverly Tyson–Smith."

The HJ moves to the whiteboard and updates: **5 guilty** votes - jurors 4, 5, 6, 9 & HJ and **2 not guilty** votes – jurors 2 & 7.

"Now we are making strides!"

Yells Juror # 4.

THE N Y CONNIVERS SERIES

37

There's a knock on the door. The Head Juror answers. The guard wheels in a cart with pastries, juices, and other snacks.
"Thank you. Instead of taking a full recess, we'll continue our deliberations through this abbreviated meal."
The guard departs. Jurors no doubt in need of a bite flock to the food cart, grab a snack, and return to their seats at the table.

THE N Y CONNIVERS SERIES

After continued deliberation, Juror # 10 casts his vote in the guilty column and tears up while doing so. Now half of the jurors are voting guilty. The HJ felt like it was going to be a slam dunk with only a few jurors in opposition. So, she continues to press.

It wasn't long before the guard returned and cleared the trash off the conference table.

There wasn't much debate from jurors 3 and 6,8, they had not said much. Juror # 12 said much but still undecided.

The debate continued. The Head Juror looked hastened to get a verdict. She respected Judge Thomas' rulings. The way he managed overruling and sustaining both the defense and the prosecution's questioning decisions of the witnesses. Feeling she had an obligation to not only deliver but to make the judge feel she was well suited for the job. With that much respect cemented and now plastered during this lengthy deliberation, she dug in.

Juror # 12 seemed like a big fish running away with the hook, line, and sinker tugging at its gills. Her reluctance to cast her vote was by now an indication she wanted to be like a sponge soaking up every bit of the debate before saying yea or nay.

So, the Head Juror targeted Juror # 8. As a construction worker, this juror seemed like he brought his hard hat into the deliberation. He argued

there was not enough evidence to convict Beverly Tyson–Smith of committing suicide., on the other hand, not enough evidence to have placed the defendants at the murder scene.

Juror # 4 although he already cast his vote, suggested Juror # 8 stop dancing around and not supportive of the process. Juror # 8, in the meantime, had some choice words for the juror, causing the HJ to step in as a referee and pour water into that conflict.

Realizing it was not the opportune time to ask for a vote of Juror # 8, she solicited the vote of Juror # 3.

Juror # 3 argued both Beverly Tyson–Smith and Brad Smith - were responsible for whatever transpired in their relationship. She argued their whole life was nothing but a façade; masked to pacify those who knew them or came in contact with them.

Additionally, Juror # 3 stated: The school Principal, Mr. Matthews, who testified in court on their behalf, gave a toast at their wedding and held them in such high esteem, saw nothing but puppy love between them two.

At ages 13 and 15, what do two high school kids know about loving each other so romantically? Some of us are grown and still drifting on the shores of love and togetherness. We are still confused as to why the bee goes to the flower.

THE N Y CONNIVERS SERIES

Noel Pendergrass, offering to take the opportunity to give them a ride home when they were drunk and vulnerable, in her eyes was morally wrong. She believed that the decision could have paved the way for Beverly's murder. Yet, Juror # 3 refrained from casting her vote at this time.

The HJ then asked Juror # 12, if she was ready to vote. To which she said "No." Claiming she needed more time to come to a decision.

With nowhere else to turn for votes the HJ revisited Juror # 8 for his decision. Was it ripe? She felt he had cooled his temperament and therefore could be easily coerced. If not she was prepared to squeeze it out of him. He asked for experiment # 2 the murder weapon. When it was delivered he argued the victim's motive for purchasing a gun. "Was it for her death or to kill someone else?"

He asked.

Additionally, he argued:

"I don't think the detectives should have arrested the defendants without enough credible evidence. If my wife were murdered and the police showed up at the door of a hotel where I was staying, of course, I would be nervously confused."

Juror # 4 took offense to his arguments and rolled his eyes.

THE N Y CONNIVERS SERIES

Juror # 8 continued: "Cops are meant to do a job and a darn great job. Even so, more times than not they construct a botched job landing innocent people in prison. No wonder…"

Juror # 4 once again retaliated against Juror # 8's talking points. Mainly the latter with a blank to fill in. Without hesitation, he charged at Juror # 8 and almost engaged in a scuffle. This time, the HJ refereed with the assistance of multiple jurors. As Juror # 8 reclaimed his seat. He said:

"Madam Head Juror, the defendants are not guilty." Once again, Juror # 4 charged Juror # 8 and had to be restrained by the other 11 jurors. This time the Guard rushed inside to investigate after the calm prevailed.

THE N Y CONNIVERS SERIES

38

The Head Juror ambled to the whiteboard and updated the stats: Guilty 6 with Not Guilty 3. Subsequently, Juror's # 3 and # 6 cast their votes in the non-guilty column. With the stat 6-5, all eyes focused on Juror # 12.

"What if we wound up with a hung jury?"
Asked Juror # 2.

"We'll inform the Judge and would have to start the process all over again."
Says HJ.
"I'm not going through this again for God's sake."
Says Juror # 4.
The HJ sensing such a possibility immediately asked Juror # 12 for her vote. The juror wavered.
 Juror # 4 interjected: "Miss Head Juror? I'm sorry for all the trouble I've caused. I should have known better. Summing up the evidence mixed with common sense. I remove all bias and withdraw my guilty vote."
"Are you sure you want to vote not guilty?"
Asks the HJ.
"I am positive. The defendants could not have committed this murder."
The other 10 jurors are surprised. Now the stats have flipped: Guilty 5 and Not Guilty 6. Juror # 12 is still holding out.
"Juror # 12 do you still need additional time?"
Asked the Head Juror, concerningly.
Juror # 12 gets up from her seat and makes eye contact with the other jurors:
"No. I know where I stand and have been all along. Brad Smith and Tessa Santos are not guilty of the murder of Beverly Tyson–Smith."
The Head Juror reiterates:

THE N Y CONNIVERS SERIES

"The verdict is in!

LATER On, Late Breaking News: *A short while ago in the Southern District Court of New York: Brad Smith and Tessa Santos were acquitted. They walked away unscathed per the verdict by 12 Jurors. This verdict was much of a surprise to many, especially in the media who felt they were accomplices in the murder of Brad Smith's ex-wife – Beverly Tyson – Smith last Spring. Meanwhile, in other related News: The gunman has been arrested for shooting at Samuel Taliaferro and Calista Cochran, the two defense attorneys who represented Smith and Santos in that trial. The two lawyers were shot at returning to the courthouse a few weeks ago. As we stated previously they walked away without a scratch.*

THE N Y CONNIVERS SERIES

THE N Y CONNIVERS SERIES

LOUISE DIPSON THE PREDATOR
TABLE OF CONTENTS

CHAPTER ONE...148
CHAPTER TWO...153
CHAPTER THREE...157
CHAPTER FOUR..160
CHAPTER FIVE..163
CHAPTER SIX...167
CHAPTER SEVEN...172
CHAPTER EIGHT...175
CHAPTER NINE..177
CHAPTER TEN...180
CHAPTER ELEVEN..183
CHAPTER TWELVE..186
CHAPTER THIRTEEN..189
CHAPTER FOURTEEN..192
CHAPTER FIFTEEN...195
CHAPTER SIXTEEN...198
CHAPTER SEVENTEEN...201
CHAPTER EIGHTEEN..205
CHAPTER NINETEEN..208
CHAPTER TWENTY..211
CHAPTER TWENTY ONE..215
CHAPTER TWENTY TWO..218
CHAPTER TWENTY THREE..222
CHAPTER TWENTY FOUR...227
CHAPTER TWENTY FIVE...231
CHAPTER TWENTY SIX..234
CHAPTER TWENTY SEVEN..237
CHAPTER TWENTY EIGHT..240
CHAPTER TWENTY NINE...243
CHAPTER THIRTY..246
CHAPTER THIRTY ONE..249
CHAPTER THIRTY TWO..252
CHAPTER THIRTY THREE..255
CHAPTER THIRTY FOUR...259
CHAPTER THIRTY FIVE...262
CHAPTER THIRTY SIX..265
CHAPTER THIRTY SEVEN..269
CHAPTER THIRTY EIGHT..272
CHAPTER THIRTY NINE...275
CHAPTER FORTY...278
CHAPTER FORTY ONE...281

THE N Y CONNIVERS SERIES

1

Sirens crescendo throughout Williamsburg, New York. This close-knit commune cliff-hanging the Boroughs of Queens, Manhattan, and Brooklyn reverberates with the noise of calamitic proportions. Setting that populous on edge.
The McDonalds' parking lot now the focal point of the calamity is inundated with Sheriff's cars, NYPD cruisers, and artillery.

THE N Y CONNIVERS SERIES

Mixed with the cries of neighbors, patrons, and friends the people cluster in multiple animated huddles. Some swearing. Some disorganized. Some dumbfounded. Others discombobulated. Powwows cut like a two-edged sword.

"She just left the house to grab a six-piece Chicken McNuggets, French fries, and a soda. That's all. Now she's missing…gone. I can't believe someone did this to Deslyn. She never bothered anyone."

Says her mother Dorothy mortified with tearful eyes and slippery cheeks.

"Whoever did this to our little Maddy will pay the consequence. Why did it take the police so long to get here? They could have prevented this…They are never on time when you need them."

Shadow the other parent Alecia Soprano. Also, in tears and showing photos of Deslyn on a busted screen iPhone with one hand and waving the other aerially seeking justice and empathy.

Meanwhile, in that now merging former huddle, Maddy's mother is engrossed in conversation with Detective Jonathan Hobbs and Detective Jamie Johnson states:

"She doesn't do any drugs…None at all! Why? What are you implying? Who is behind this…?"

THE N Y CONNIVERS SERIES

In the meantime, friends, and neighbors, in yet another cluster share their concerns.

"They were only thirteen and fourteen years old." Voiced another rattled neighbor as she paces back and forth and then circles multiple huddled acquaintances. While holding on tightly to the hand of her young teen daughter.

Other frantic teens converge. Some chaperoned, some unsupervised, others unleashed. Seemingly, the leader in that pack was a tall and slender girl with amber, green hair and displaying her total independence with hand gestures. She chimes in verbally:

"Dessie and Maddy are my BFF's...Totally for life! They never got into any trouble. Why did someone have to do such an injustice? Why did anyone...? Why? Please, somebody, help me understand. This is an unlawful act not only on my friends but on our community. That's why I'll be attending law school after I graduate from Williamsburg High! The Senate is falling asleep at their posts. It's time to get these predators off our streets. I shall! I must!"

Detectives Hobbs and Johnson are now engaged in the questioning of a uniformed green-bloused-khaki pants McDonald's employee. She walks out of the restaurant terrified and still trembling like a leaf. Her name tag reads Arlene Gomez – Shift Manager. "Yes.

THE N Y CONNIVERS SERIES

The two girls after being served walked out of the restaurant. First, they contemplated eating in. One of them said it's way too hot and congested inside this joint. And then they bounced…I mean, they headed out the door. They were glued to their smartphones, texting like crazy."

"Who served them?" Asked Det. Johnson. "It was I. I did…They were acting weird. One said she wanted a chocolate shake then changed her mind to vanilla after being served."

Said the Shift Manager.

Meanwhile, additional Law Enforcement in marked and unmarked vehicles arrive in droves. Even some ambulances join their convoys. The two lead detectives Hobbs and Johnson press alertly for answers to these missing teens' dilemma. It was clear to them the only eyewitness was Arlene Gomez. Multiple parents, some seemingly preoccupied with their after-work chores bear down, reacting to the news.

"Shortly after they came outside."

The Manager continued…

"In a flash, a midnight blue SUV pulled up. The front door opened. They were thrown inside through the rear door. The vehicle took off speedily. That's all I saw. OMG! Why did this have to happen on my watch?"

THE N Y CONNIVERS SERIES

Still trembling,

"Did you get a glimpse of the license tags or the driver, anybody?"

Asked Detective Hobbs still grilling Arlene Gomez.

"No. I did not. Everything seemed to happen so fast like a scene from a Spider-Man movie. By the time it registered, the vehicle sped away leaving smoke and the sound of squealing tires in our parking lot. Just like that, it was gone. Gone through those back streets." Detective Johnson radios:

"A Midnight blue SUV, over! With freshly peeled tires. Make and model unidentified!"

Multiple once-parked police vehicles abandon the parking lot in haste and careen through increasing gridlocked street traffic. Meanwhile, several onlookers continually vent:

"She knows who did it. This is such a cover-up!" Pointing to the fast-food outlet.

THE N Y CONNIVERS SERIES

2

With the getaway fresh in the air. Law Enforcement pounced with a warlike demeanor. They set up roadblocks along major streets throughout Williamsburg, stretching across the bridge to Delancey Street and extending towards the Holland Tunnel and on selective Manhattan streets.

THE N Y CONNIVERS SERIES

Also, strategically within the Five Boroughs. Ultimately, they concentrated a heavy police presence on the viaducts leading up to the Lincoln Tunnel and George Washington Bridge on the New York City sides.

Secondly, the Verrazano Bridge connecting Brooklyn with Staten Island was targeted as yet another checkpoint.

Thirdly, they sat up checkpoints at the entrances to both John F. Kennedy and La Guardia airports. Discussion among the lead detectives mounted in the case. Hobbs and Johnson announced their concerns surrounding the Staten Island and New Jersey pass. Consequently, the Belt Parkway East and West suffered tremendous traffic gridlock along with major streets flowing into this shoreline parkway wrapping around the coastal portion of Brooklyn.

The traffic alerts sent to New Yorkers' cell phones read "Very strong police presence around the Belt Parkway East and West of the Verrazano Bridge. Avoid it at all costs."

The New York Mayor made some subsequent remarks urging New Yorkers to avoid certain gridlock traffic routes and if they see something, please say something. In addition to these checkpoints at major New York airports, a strong National Guard presence complimented, flaunting

THE N Y CONNIVERS SERIES

their assault rifles. They were destined to trap this predator.

Meanwhile, multiple SUVs painted midnight blue became under vicious scrutiny. Many motorists driving identifying utility vehicles were pulled over, questioned and vehicles searched. While these motorists underwent such inquiry, some of the questions raised to them included:

"Where are you heading to? Have you been through Williamsburg in the last ten hours?"

Displaying signs detailing profiles of the victims: "Have you seen these two girls in the last ten hours? Have you seen another SUV in this same color subverting traffic?"

All those questions mounted as Mt. Everest within the investigation.

Law Enforcement understood though: typically, anyone with an SUV that color would normally detect one similar even though not in the same make and model. Anything to connect the dots. It was universally understood motorists are conditioned to detect other autos in their league.

The Newsflash on Cable TV stations as well as Network TV and even Radio, sounded like a broken record throughout that Friday night's already scheduled programs and continuing into early Saturday morning newscasts: *If you see a suspicious*

THE N Y CONNIVERS SERIES

midnight blue SUV. Please say something by calling the NYPD immediately. **800-577-TIPS.**

THE N Y CONNIVERS SERIES

3

With limited information on the identity of this runaway predator. Law enforcement was caught handicapped in their expedition. Bringing in the suspect seemed like a mountainous climb without corroborating imagery or even a criminal backstory. Even so, they were determined to find answers. Any SUV that looked

THE N Y CONNIVERS SERIES

like or smelled like the getaway vehicle, uniformed police pulled over in their quest to solve this criminal outrage.

At the stroke of midnight on Saturday, a little over 24 hours since Maddy St. Hilaire and Deslyn Soprano disappeared from the Williamsburg neighborhood, NYPD officers pulled over and searched many suspicious SUVs. In particular, one along the Bronx River Parkway, bolting towards the George Washington Bridge.

Inside this vehicle, they discovered and seized multiple rifles along with other ammunition. That motorist was also questioned and detained. This motorist claimed he worked with New York Corrections and was transporting weapons to Rikers. When pressed for his badge and ID, he claimed he rushed out of the house forgetting them. They slapped cuffs on him and later impounded the vehicle.

By early morning, Sunday his vehicle was swept. It turned up clean of any of the girl's DNA. Reportedly, calls came in from the correction department: their driver was returning to base at Rikers after a seizure. Even though he was IDed by those officers. They were not leaving anything up to chance.

THE N Y CONNIVERS SERIES

Their quest to catch this predator before he or she struck again like a sore wound was fermenting and smelled - urgent.

A short time thereafter, additional news in the case surfaced. Subsequently, Arlene Gomez, McDonald's first responder was questioned deeper by Hobbs, and Johnson at the precinct.

"The Predator was fully masked who pulled off the abduction of those two teenagers."

Arlene Gomez recalled. Subsequently, that McDonald's fast food restaurant surveillance camera was played back. Ironically, there was no surveillance footage to support the crime. "Very odd!" complained Detective Johnson. All that non-information, thrown into the mix consequently presented a severe challenge for this investigation with this predator still at large. Meanwhile, fingers still pointed at Arlene Gomez. Not only in the media but also in the Williamsburg community. "Did she have anything to do with the crime? Was she complicit? Was she a cover-up in this abduction?" were some of the concerns raised. Subsequently, Arlene Gomez was arrested on suspicion charges of this twin abduction of young teen girls.

THE N Y CONNIVERS SERIES

4

As a result of Friday night's tragedy, parents began reigning in their young teens-girls by 7:00 PM. On Monday night, exactly three nights after the Williamsburg hit. Bedford-Stuyvesant, Brooklyn was also victimized. The third girl in this abduction string was nabbed.

THE N Y CONNIVERS SERIES

Marlene Monroe, a fifteen-year-old girl was snatched outside Fulton Street and Nostrand Avenue Mall. Onlookers described what they witnessed during that lightning-speed abduction: Someone with moves like a woman and masked fleeing the street in mint green Land Rover.

After corroborating statements made by an onlooker, who once again was unable to capture the vehicle's temporary tags. It seemed like the same scenario explained to the lead detectives. In an interview with CNN, Detectives Hobbs and Johnson begged to differ. "Copycats don't act like that. This is too dangerous a crime for someone fearing such incriminating scrutiny by the 'red alerted' NYPD to emulate. This by far seems like the actions of a sole proprietor."

Said the flustered detective Jamie Johnson.

Now on high alert, the NYPD dispatched convoys from their fleet throughout Bedford-Stuyvesant and other neighboring communities. While some still claimed it was a copycat incident, Hobbs and Johnson weren't sharing those sentiments. They pressed the entire NYPD department for assistance. It did not only escalate with those two cops' pursuit but the parents of now all three teens pressured their neighbors to write their senators and congressmen

for help in capturing this minuscule yet insufficiently unidentified predator.

Some news reporting legal scholars reasoned
 "Now that another similar or related incident has occurred. Copycat or not. Law enforcement could be placed in a state of confusion. Not only are they in search of a midnight blue SUV without identifiable license tags but they are also looking for a mint-green Land Rover with unidentifiable tags. Plus, there is very little info on the identity of the predator. What role is the DMV playing in all of this?"
In response, Law enforcement claimed their street cameras might finally turn up images of any of those two vehicles. Plus, any other abductions could be hindered.
 "They need to update those cameras. They are probably outdated. Thus, it is only good at catching motorists who run the red light. That's all."
Said a concerned Williamsburg parent.
Meanwhile, Arlene Gomez, the shift manager at McDonald's in Williamsburg was released from police custody. Law enforcement realized the abduction spree was very much still alive while Gomez sat.

THE N Y CONNIVERS SERIES

5

It has now been more than a week since the first abduction occurred inside that McDonald's parking lot. Yet, at this point, no arrests were made. With the identity of the predator still unmasked. Several entities close to the case remained on edge hoping they could easily slice into this pent-up case.

THE N Y CONNIVERS SERIES

While the search was concentrated in NYC and those connecting cities toward New Jersey, the FBI embarked on a nationwide search. Most airports were heavily armed now even Newark Airport in New Jersey and Bradley International in Connecticut with attack dogs, assault weaponry State Troopers, the military, and even the Army's National Guards. In a sense, it was metaphorically going to war domestically versus that predator like none before.

In the meantime, up and down the Hudson River police helicopters and speedboats roamed.

"Whoever started this was going to pay."

Said Hobbs lead detective on the case to a low-level officer echoing the wish of New York's Mayor. On the other hand, many other cops low on the totem pole and inundated with constant street patrol showed much frustration in body language and attitude.

LATER, at a gas station in White Plains, a midnight blue SUV in question pulled up to refuel. The station attendant in her twenties but looking like eighteen to look younger, instinctively reached for the phone and began dialing.

She dialed 911 before aborting the call as the driver attired NYPD uniform walked inside, laid a $100 bill on the counter, and said:

THE N Y CONNIVERS SERIES

"I need a full tank on pump number nine"
The attendant still rattled but much less than when the vehicle pulled up alongside the pump and that motorist put that crisp Franklin on the counter. She quickly dispatched the note in her drawer and nervously entertained the other customer in the line. The attendant remained puzzled.
"Is this a man or a woman?"
She questioned under her breath.
Meanwhile, the motorist sauntered towards the pump island. At pump number nine, the motorist pumped almost $95.00 in the vehicle's empty tank and kept on pumping until the entire $100 worth was consumed. Returning to the driver's seat a brawl broke out with one of the passengers. Madly, the driver dispenses a sharp uppercut followed by a left jab on the attacker. Screams erupted with different tempos. With the driver's window half-cocked, the attacker a teen girl chilled. The eavesdropping attendant peripherally witnessed and overheard those excruciating altercations to the opponent's head.
Immediately, the attendant grabbed the telephone receiver, reached into her drawer, and scanned the 100-dollar bill. Realizing it was fake, she instantly dialed 911. By this time, the vehicle had already departed from the gas station. Westchester County

THE N Y CONNIVERS SERIES

police arrived minutes later but there was no one to buttonhole. Multiple $25,000.00 rewards signs plastered NYC.

6

The predator had now for the first time left some breadcrumbs for the ravens who were aggressively tailing. The gas station attendant told them everything she overheard and witnessed. So, as the news spread like a California brush fire with nationwide proportions, law enforcement was busily putting the pieces together all evening and

THE N Y CONNIVERS SERIES

night long to produce a plausible strategy for their continued woman hunt.

During the early morning hours of the next day, the North Shore of Long Island was swarmed with cops as two bodies believed to be those of Maddy St. Hilaire and Deslyn Soprano lay on the beach. It was alleged they had washed ashore. Their bodies seemed brutally mutilated and concussion saturated. According to Detective Jamie Johnson at the crime scene:

"It looked like someone had not only used them as punching bags but according to their torn attire had viciously raped and strangled them."

Police helicopters littered the sky and coast guard boats swarmed the seas from the coast of Long Island to Connecticut – catching nothing in their nets. It was now very apparent this investigation had turned into an escalated dilemma. Detectives Hobbs and Johnson embarked on the scene and tarried way after sunset. It was at dusk when they received a call: It was from the medical examiner who seemed to have worked overtime. The autopsy conducted on both girls revealed stunning perceptions.

"Whoever carried this out knows how to punch adeptly. Their trajectory was consistent with left jabs, right jabs, upper-cut, and flush. The concussions seemed as if they were administered by a man with

huge fists. We'll be working overnight to provide full discovery."

This seemed like an unusual cliff-hanging autopsy. Meanwhile, Detective Johnson spoke with a reporter and dropped this message:

"We need to act sooner than later. Any one of these girls could have been your sister or mine." While the search for this mysterious predator continued, and law enforcement homed in on Long Island, the FBI went gleaning through other nearby cities. A tip led them to White Plains. Every known Boxing Ring was visited and searched for any possible forensic or DNA linking to these teens, along with any evidence to verify if the predator had been in the system. After three days of searching, there was no, there, there.

However, on day five of their expedition post the two girls' bodies washed up on Long Islands' North Shore, the FBI raided a Chop Shop in White Plains, New York. There were no clues that a midnight blue SUV nor a mint green Land Rover had passed through that automobile butchery.

The Feds walked away loaded with three employees of that establishment in handcuffs, computers, cell phones, and loads of cash. Backdropped with a chained door as well as a parking lot. They loaded them into vans and departed.

THE N Y CONNIVERS SERIES

Three arrests nonetheless but this did not spin well in the media. Why were they arresting Chop Shop pundits while this predator was still at large? Sparking a rift between the Feds and the two Lead detectives. As to whose case it was, and the linkage of arrests that only had to do with the case. The credits became a toss-up between these two entities.
"At least, if the Feds were going to make those kinds of off-the-beaten-path arrests, they should securely keep them under wraps so as not to aggravate the lead detectives on the case. "
Anyway, Trump was never indicted as of yet for any of his crimes but multiple offenders inside his clique were."
Stated one legal expert in the Feds' defense.
"They know how to function lawfully."
Reasoned the Teen Advocate from the Williamsburg crime scene. Knowingly, botched arrests have not only plagued the NYPD but stigmatized and infested it. For example, the choking death of Eric Garner in Staten Island and multiple most recent mishaps. This certainly cast a shadow on crimefighting globally as well as sprinkling salt inside the wound as far as NYC was concerned. Even though the police had an agenda to get this predator off the streets. Many civilians were very reluctant to provide any assistance that could help them in their

THE N Y CONNIVERS SERIES

investigations. Except for the victim's parents, well-wishers, and an eclectic group upholding the right arm of justice.

THE N Y CONNIVERS SERIES

7

While the Westchester County gas station attendant swore on the Bible it was a possible transvestite attired Cop she saw walking inside the station. Placed a one hundred dollar bill on the counter and said: *fill up!* walked back to the pump side, filled it up with gas, and drove away after a brawl broke out inside the SUV.

THE N Y CONNIVERS SERIES

While in a statement-collecting mode. Hobbs and Johnson received the remainder of the autopsy report for the two murdered teen girls Maddy St. Hilaire and Deslyn Soprano. Now conclusively, the report upped the story.

They refocused on the gas station attendant's account. However, that's all she wrote. All the information that the attendant captured in her confused state of mind before that assailant bounced, hitting the streets of Westchester.

Consequently, many pondered inside the media: If the predator was a male or most likely a female NYC cop who showed up at that Westchester gas station, she had accomplices rendering her bidding - working as a team or enterprise. Indicating law enforcement was missing multiple clues along the way. Even though their talking point was:

"Catch this predator before he or she strikes again."

There was no image profile of this predator still at large. Instead, posted signs read: The predator was last seen posing as a male and now they are saying a female NYPD officer. Although this was a step in the right direction it had dire consequences referencing a female cop. This idea selectively confused the heck out of female officers trying to do their jobs unshielded by a male partner.

THE N Y CONNIVERS SERIES

Plus, with that alleged female persona acting like a cop and published in the media. An uncalculated move: any smart perpetrator will be otherwise prompted to change their propriety to prey on others undetected or from a standpoint of authority.

Meanwhile, in the mid-afternoon of that same day, another teen, the fourth, was abducted outside a recreation park. This time in Rochester, New York, and further north. This escalation left the two lead detectives scratching their heads.

THE N Y CONNIVERS SERIES

8

One thing was clear to the lead detectives: Whoever was carrying out these abductions was flying low under the radar. With only that tidbit of information to this point. They felt they were aggressively looking for a needle in a haystack. "We have to talk to people. We can't expect them to come to us. We have to focus on being proactive.

THE N Y CONNIVERS SERIES

Them giving us a hand could be farfetched." Said Johnson during a Cable TV interview.

"Parents are scared. Teens are humiliated. Sometimes it might be a stretch reaching out to us but we're here for you. We are here for your community. Please if you see something, say something and we promise you we'll do the rest."

Said Hobbs in a tone as if he were running for the Mayorship. Inside local barbershops and salons, the strategy of cops now needing the help of their communities was widely discussed. Although the commune was bleeding from the pain inflicted by this predator, many not trusting the cops were prepared to wear a band-aid on this new wound even if it hurts them. Yep. That Eric Gardener's innocent killing like a thorn in their side still pricked them every time the cops said: "We need your help." It was by now a given Law enforcement needed the public on board to aid their investigation. As sophisticated as their weaponry and intel, they had to solicit the help of civilians – boots on the ground. Many civilians felt the chasm between them and law enforcement for way too long had been a one-way street. Removing that street sign would no doubt be a start toward ending the chaotic infrastructure between the police and civilians.

THE N Y CONNIVERS SERIES

9

Hours later, that autopsy expanded report surprisingly revealed: Sperm was found in the genital area of both girls. According to the tests, the substance differed associated with both teens. Possibly transferred from two different men. Focused on the written report, Hobbs looked across at Johnson, puzzled.

THE N Y CONNIVERS SERIES

"Now the thought of a criminal serial enterprise looms large. There's pluralism."
He echoes.
Corroborating their findings, many pondered: If the predator was a female who had the audacity to disguise as an NYC cop, and who showed up at that Westchester County gas station. Was there a possible impersonator on their hands? Or were there copycats? They queried. She must have accomplices rendering her bidding - working as a team or enterprise insisted detective Johnson. Signifying law enforcement was missing some clues along the way and not closer to an arrest.
Even though one of their talking points was:
Catch this predator before he or she strikes again.
They lacked the competence to wheel her in. Playing catch up distantly, unfortunately, was in their DNA. By now acquired no image profile of this predator still at large. Instead, posted signs read: The predator was last seen posing as a female NYPD officer. Yet, there was concrete evidence regarding sexual origin or gender.
"They were still malnourished evidentially."
Said the Teen Advocate, wannabe attorney from Williamsburg to an interviewer.
"Anybody could acquire a cop's uniform if they decided to play a bad actor."

THE N Y CONNIVERS SERIES

Said, Detective Jonathan Hobbs without genuinely weighing the shortcomings of that statement. How? Although this sounded like it had validity it had dire consequences. This idea confused the heck out of female officers trying to do their jobs properly. Plus, with that alleged persona acting like a cop and published in the media resembled an uncalculated move. Why? Any smart perpetrator would be otherwise prompted to change their propriety to prey on their victim undetected.

Meanwhile, in the mid-afternoon on that same day, another teen was abducted outside a recreation park. Now the fourth abduction so far. This time in Rochester, New York, further north. This escalation left the lead detectives scratching their heads. Evident there were so many questions yet very few answers.

THE N Y CONNIVERS SERIES

10

While law enforcement expanded their hunt in upstate New York for the predator, news broke: The Gas Station attendant from that Westchester County gas station was now missing apparently abducted on her way home. Later that evening, the lone onlooker came forward, stating the attendant was waiting at the bus

stop when the incident went down. Also vouching that the hit was conducted by a Caucasian-looking woman wearing an afro hairstyle as was described in the earlier abduction in White Plains.

Once again, it was reported: This abduction now the fifth like the others happened fast and furious. The onlooker was unable to recall much else, except it all, went down swiftly.

Westchester County police jointly with Hobbs and Johnson were busily putting the pieces together while conferring with other NYC agencies as well as the FBI. By sunrise, law enforcement had encamped at a vacant parking lot where the gas station attendant's body was discovered, brutally mutilated, raped, and deep concussions to the face and head like what the other victims suffered.

Not since serial killer William Devon Howell, described as the drifter prowled in nearby Connecticut streets in 2003. Where he roamed the streets in his van dubbed his "murder mobile" did the Tri-State of New York, New Jersey and Connecticut encounter such brutal murderous seriality.

By then, not much-aided law enforcement in bringing down this predator. Howell back in 2003 had abducted, assaulted, and murdered seven

THE N Y CONNIVERS SERIES

people who he buried in his garden behind a strip mall as a memorial.

Now, although a strong police presence remained in upstate New York. In less than five hours after the body of the gas station attendant was discovered, the body of the third victim from that Brooklyn Mall was discovered in a dense field in Westchester, New York. According to detective Jonathan Hobbs when he heard the news:

"Now it seems like that predator is acting as a killer on steroids and must be immediately stopped."

11

Later that evening. Responding to a tip out of Bethpage, Long Island. Detectives Hobbs and Johnson pulled up outside a house perched in a cul-de-sac with a mint-green Land Rover parked in its descendent driveway. The home was partially lit, and the sunset was already history. Hobbs knocked first, then kicked the door in and entered in

THE N Y CONNIVERS SERIES

takedown style. Johnson provided cover. As Hobbs entered the house, a backup SWAT team encamped in front of the house. Going through the side door and trying to get away, a slim and slender elderly man was trapped and commanded to drop his weapon. He retaliated at first but then expediently obliged. He was handcuffed and his Maranda rights read to him by detective Jamie Johnson.

Johnson shoved him inside on the rear seat of their Sedan. Moments later, the mint-green Land Rover was towed away from the driveway.

About an hour later, at the police station, Hobbs administered very strong interrogation tactics on the man who we now learned was Antonio Calderon, a man of Italian heritage and an ex-police officer with the NYPD. However, he checked out clean without any criminal past.

It seemed Calderon embellished having his rights read to him at his arrest as he thereafter remained tightlipped as if he very much intended on pleading the fifth.

The Land Rover was thoroughly swept and hair particles of that third victim abducted from the Brooklyn Mall were lifted. Additionally, semen found thus far on and inside the bodies of three of four deceased victims matched Calderon's DNA. Detectives Hobbs and Johnson felt certain based on

THE N Y CONNIVERS SERIES

evidence they had found one of their men, except Calderon refused to fess-up. According to the detectives he elected to remain tongue-tied.

If it wasn't for the semen found on the other girl's body, which proved different from Calderon's, the detectives might have cooled their heels upon his arrest.

THE N Y CONNIVERS SERIES

12

For days on end, the news reverberated and spun in multiple rhetorical theoretical directions. "One down! They caved! They can run but they can't hide!" was the word on the streets. In the meantime, candlelight vigils in multiple communities, including Westchester County multiplied as mourners celebrated their dead. Counter-terrorism taskforce, as well as law

THE N Y CONNIVERS SERIES

enforcement entities, camped out at related sites for precautionary measures.

Early the following morning, tragedy struck once again. This time in Mt. Vernon, New York, where two teen girls were abducted in broad daylight outside Mt. Vernon High School. Victims now tolling seven. It was later discovered: School surveillance camera harnessed on the school, and which was supposed to be operable wasn't. Same scenario to the occurrence at that Williamsburg McDonalds.

Back on the hunt were detectives Hobbs and Johnson. They speedily embarked on Mt. Vernon looking for much-needed answers. All they got was suppositions and maybes. Some people claimed they saw the vehicle speeding through their neighborhood and like greased lightning it disappeared. As Hobbs previously predicted:

"This predator is not a lone wolf going after our sheep. There's a team, a clique, an enterprise, and we've got to ax them. This may be a team effort but not bigger than us. We're the finest. The NYPD. We have standards to uphold – the highest."

In hindsight, it finally dawned on Hobbs that Calderon was too frail and slender, plus as an elderly man, he could not possibly land those alleged punches afflicted on those victims. Plus, he was small fisted, to say the least. Hobbs' awakening to this fact

THE N Y CONNIVERS SERIES

came after an additional autopsy report claimed one of the victims suffered a broken collar bone from a possible laden punch in the neck region.

Meanwhile, Johnson was still whispering in Hobbs's ear what should be done to Antonio Calderon for preying on these young girls. It was a chemically harsh punishment. She even entertained the idea of firstly dusting off her karate skills on the elderly Calderon. Seemingly, he was elated preying on these young girls. She even claimed he was a centerfold torn out of Jeffrey Epstein's playbook.

THE N Y CONNIVERS SERIES

13

A t this stage of the investigation. An inquiry that began a little over two weeks ago in Williamsburg. Five teen girls were already abducted and murdered with their remains recovered. With two other teens unaccounted for. One perpetrator, Antonio Calderon, was arrested and charged. Plus, three Chop Shop employees in

THE N Y CONNIVERS SERIES

White Plains, although not charged with any of these abductions or murders but got caught up in a sweep operation pursued by the FBI, were already behind bars.

In the interim, it was clear to law enforcement, whoever was currently orchestrating these hits on young teen girls was still at large and must cease and desist.

Many calls flowed into the department's switchboard geared to bring down the predator but to no avail. Multiple baiting scenarios spun out of control in the media and people congregated just about everywhere. Now, like a complicated upside-down jig-saw puzzle, all the pieces problematically didn't fit. Why? The probabilities regarding the true identity of the predator were still oblivious.

Even law enforcement, although not admittedly felt the uncanniness of the crime they were investigating. Some cops during their coffee breaks envisioned the investigation as a reincarnated Sherlock Holmes experience.

Additionally, Calderon's protectiveness to remain tight-lipped was distressing the detectives. There were no cell phone records to track his paths as no phone was recovered upon his arrest.

THE N Y CONNIVERS SERIES

Finally, synchronically a tip dropped. The lead detectives sensed they had collaboratively hit a home run.

At the latest abduction, it was reported: A police camera located on Main Street captured a profile of the villain adorned wearing a blonde wig while attempting that last getaway. This image was speedily transmitted to detectives Hobbs and Johnson at police headquarters and expediently distributed to every law enforcement agency in NYC. It was almost dark, and they wanted to take advantage of whatever daylight remained. Plus, a slight chance of snow was forecasted, and the weatherman jinxing Mother Nature; the area got blanketed. So, the night passed without another strike by the predator.

THE N Y CONNIVERS SERIES

14

E arly next morning before the crack of dawn, and snowplows were still active, cops, like flies on molasses swarmed the streets of Westchester County looking for the predator. The name headlined their thinking - **Louise Dipson** an ex-NYPD officer. Her profile reportedly matched the

THE N Y CONNIVERS SERIES

description of the predator, connected in pulling off the abductees, rapes, and murders of those innocent teen girls. Detectives Hobbs and Johnson were confident; they now had something tangible to latch onto – a suspect. Most of all they were confident this was their woman and were resolute in stopping her before she struck again. They became heavy-footed.
Paradoxically, Hobbs sensed he was served a half-baked cake. Realizing the gooeyness, he demanded the entire profile on Dipson. It seemed as if someone or a clique at the 71st Precinct in Brooklyn located at New York Avenue and Empire Blvd had suppressed most of Dipson's information. Hobbs' detective partner Jamie Johnson read in and questioned:
"Why is this a drip, drip? What the hell are they hiding?"
"This seems like a total cover-up."
Responded Jonathan Hobbs.
It now hurried up and waited.
Hobbs got on his cell phone, reached out to their captain demanding Louise Dipson's entire profile. The stalled process was overturned when the captain intervened and later texted Hobbs, but it was still drip, drip.
Louise Dipson worked at the NYPD in *Crown Heights*... Yet, her connections were missing. Clearly, her profile was on lockdown. Hobbs and Johnson

THE N Y CONNIVERS SERIES

once again LOUISE DIPSON (THE PREDATOR) 51 51 demanded her entire profile and nothing less. Who she knew, who knew her, everything? The Governor of New York was alerted and pressured the NYPD into coughing up Dipson's entire Bio. Challenged, the team of Connivers at that precinct though hesitantly, complied with the Governor's escalated demand.

THE N Y CONNIVERS SERIES

15

Louise Dipson's profile was rapidly unraveling in the media and elsewhere. More so than the Robert Mueller Report. *Louise Dipson was born to devout Catholic parents. They resided in Crown Heights, New York. A community mostly inhabited by orthodox Jews. Louise attended high school during those days of the Crown Height riots.*

THE N Y CONNIVERS SERIES

It was during the tenure when NYC elected the first black mayor – Mr. Dinkins. When Dinkin's term was at a low ebb, and the prosecutor from the Southern District Court of New York – Giuliani decided to challenge Dinkins for the mayorship and won. Louise Dipson joined the NYPD. Her days prior to high school proved one to be reckoned with. She very seldom associated with the girls in her class and categorized them as weak. If you wanted to find her, look for where the boys spent time together and there she was. Playing everything from 3-card-Monty and other trick games. Louise played all the sports. You name the game and she enlisted. On evenings after school, she frequented the boxing rings in Brooklyn. Although underaged to enter most of those facilities, she adopted the art of talking her way in, over, around, and out of situations. The guys loved hanging out with Louise and nicknamed her "The Dip." One evening a brawl broke out after a boxing event. It was between two of the guys with whom she frequently spent time together. She did not only referee the fight but took down both of the guys in whose hands she could easily crumble like an unleavened pretzel. The boys thereafter set her apart as the girl no to mess with, and whichever boy group she affiliated with, they became fisted as steel. Dipson learned how to throw a punch and it landed with a thud. When she frequented the club, other women envied her. It was said: "Louise could dance her An off and men flocked to her like a magnet.

THE N Y CONNIVERS SERIES

The news descrambled and listeners and viewers became glued to their gadgets.

THE N Y CONNIVERS SERIES

16

Louise Dipson never got married. Many wondered Why? Some claimed that whoever the man was to become hitched with Louise had it coming as he would have a tussle on his hands with revenge deep-seated in her psyche. Her mother Ellen Dipson passed on when Louise was only 19

years of age, the result of a motorist mauling a pedestrian in Crown Heights.

Weeks later, the driver, a Jamaican immigrant was arrested in conjunction with the accident. He not only posted a strong defense, but onlookers testified her mother crossed the street at Utica Avenue and Eastern Parkway while the traffic light was still green. The driver claimed it was a foggy night and he was later acquitted. This didn't sit too well with Dipson even though her mother suffered from the disease Alzheimer's.

Louise remained on edge and thought the light was yellow and turning red instead of green and turning yellow as stated. That motorist, it was alleged, hauled her mother under his illegal taxi's chassis for many blocks.

"It was just before sunset on a Friday. He should have known that he was driving through a predominantly Jewish neighborhood where its residents were always rushing to complete their tasks just before sundown on Fridays, according to welcoming in the Sabbath. The bell had already chimed in Crown Heights, and he should have heard it…dah?"

She lamented.

Louise, along with her friends, mostly Jewish, organized and picketed against the upcoming West

THE N Y CONNIVERS SERIES

Indian Day parade on Eastern Parkway that year. She was successful in getting the attention of not only the predominantly Jewish community but the media as well. Protest-related signs were stapled on just about every light pole in Brooklyn.

However, the revenue generated from this event which attracted millions of tourists to NYC on Labor Day weekend far outweighed any plans to derail the Labor Day festivities. Plus, the City Council had their hands deep inside the till.

THE N Y CONNIVERS SERIES

17

Later that fall, Louise Dipson attended the Police Academy and became an NYPD officer. It wasn't long before she walked the beat in Crown Heights, with her chest stuck out and her gun visibly protruding from its holster. Always ready to cite violators of the law - she telegraphed.

THE N Y CONNIVERS SERIES

Dipson, speedily earned her stripes with the NYPD and within only a few short years, she was tapped to head up a team of officers, instrumental in bringing down a prostitution ring on Buffalo Avenue and East New York Avenue. About half a mile north of Crown Heights. For this clean sweep operation, she earned numerous accolades as the rookie cop who shook that prostitution ring loose.

Her love interest at the department was Captain Jerome Meeks, who endowed her with pleasantries. Gossiped at the department:

"Captain Meeks is single so why don't they tie the knot?"

Conversely, this truism: Familiarity breeds contempt borne out. It wasn't long before Louise Dipson was sleeping with some of those pimps, she chased off the block at Buffalo Avenue. They subsequently relocated to mid-town Manhattan and Dipson became Miss NYPD uniformed in the daytime and Pimp Daddy's pet and his play bunny at night.

Pimp Daddy, the flamboyant and classy dresser. Seen most times in a trench coat and a cigar in his mouth. One of the few men empowered to curb Louise. Instinctively, he kept her under heavy manners. The NYPD busted Louise one night as they supplanted a deep undercover unit in that newly formed Manhattan prostitution ring, the locale

THE N Y CONNIVERS SERIES

where she patronized. It was later revealed, the undercover officer offered to pay Louise much more than the going rate.

However, Jerome Meeks, oblivious to Louise Dipson shared a triangular relationship with Nicole Best, a higher-up at Internal Affairs. A conflict of interest? He clearly saw his future with Nicole Best who was known for throwing her weight around and frequented major governmental circles extended as far as Washington, DC.

Louise Dipson suddenly felt his cold shoulder. It took only a month for Internal affairs to state their findings and Louise was terminated without pay. Meanwhile, her stomach grew. Most of her peeps encouraged her to abort the fetus. Louise refused; bent on her staunch Catholic upbringings.

Her daughter Cherae Louise Dipson was born almost seven months later. Now we are still without adequate employment and a young one to take care of. Louise became penniless and resorted to welfare support. Like a sliding iceberg, she went downhill. Louise Dipson eventually collected and sold soda and beer cans.

Bouncing back, she took a job at a local supermarket bagging groceries. To her dismay, many of those violators she cited while being strapped. Subsequently, she worked her way up the ladder

THE N Y CONNIVERS SERIES

with that Supermarket giant and by the time Cherae was ready to attend high school she positioned herself as the store manager.

THE N Y CONNIVERS SERIES

18

Louise Dipson, ardently cemented deep in the annals of New York law enforcement taught her daughter whatever street smarts she deemed relevant. So much that her Cherae swaggered, cherishing being endowed with that upper hand. "Although I've never done everything my mother wanted. I'm very mindful of all that she

taught me." Those words echoed from her mother and through the fertile mind of young Cherae.

The young Dipson was a straight "A" student at Crown Heights High and seemed destined to steer her way through law school at John Jay College, upon which, she very early sat her sights as a supreme litigator. As a leader in all sports as well as the Associated Student Body she excelled. During the Parkland School shootings in Florida a few years ago, Cherae encapsulated the tragedy as:

"That will never happen in NYC. Not in my school!" Cherae bonded with a handful of students including Nikia Chavez. On one hot summer's day in July a year later, Cherae did not return from school. A search went out for days throughout the five Boroughs for the missing model student from Crown Heights High. There was not a trace. Zilch. Nada. Zip. Zero! She disappeared without a trace.

New York law enforcement hit the streets vehemently. After a week of futility, a partially decomposed girl's body was found deep in a Westchester County Park Woodlands aided by vultures.

After an autopsy, it revealed the girl's body which was brutally mutilated, with multiple stabbed wounds and evidence of rape was Cherae Dipson's. It seemed like that was water under the bridge.

THE N Y CONNIVERS SERIES

However, two years later, on what would have been Cherae's eighteenth birthday, the two teens Deslyn Soprano and Maddy St. Hilaire were abducted from the parking lot of that McDonald's fast-food restaurant in another close-knit community - Williamsburg, New York.

THE N Y CONNIVERS SERIES

19

With all that backstory in the play. The lead detectives in the investigation of the alleged predator, Hobbs, and Johnson, not only knew who they were looking for but influenced a large segment of the New York populous to call on the Governor to step up police street patrol statewide. The cover on Louise Dipson's

THE N Y CONNIVERS SERIES

Facebook page with her daughter backdropped read: An eye for an eye. A tooth for a tooth.

Several weeks after Louise Dipson began her menacing rampage on young teen girls the most intense search for her so far was conducted.

Paradoxically, it was recorded as one of the slowest nights of citations since the department was born on New Year's Day 1898.

Just after 9:00 AM the following morning, instead of dragging this predator inside their net, tragedy once again struck. This time outside a train station at Dyre Ave close to the border of the Bronx and Mt. Vernon. The final stop on the # 5 Train. All passengers on this train had already disembarked including Carla DeFreitas and Camille Glasgow, two girls in their mid-teens who mostly grouped and known as C.C.

Backpack-laden, they rushed through the turnstiles to catch the waiting bus which now became mobile leaving smoke in their faces. The two girls were frustrated with the total letdown. Dropped their guard somewhat.

Louise Dipson saw them unhinged and adeptly pounced into their space. By the time onlookers zeroed in on the unfolding scene - Dipson had already shoved the two girls inside her abduct-mobile – midnight blue SUV and drove away speedily.

THE N Y CONNIVERS SERIES

Later, one of those onlookers, who preferred to remain anonymous claimed:

"The entire episode transpired so darn fast. By the time I realized what was happening, the SUV with a hard-to-read license tag turned the corner north on Dyre Avenue and sped out of sight towards the Westchester County border. At this point, I yelled out 'Help! Somebody, please help!' No one dared.

A motorist driving an illegal taxi cab. I believe he did hear my scream for help. Instead of chasing behind the perpetrator, he headed in the opposite direction. Reading his lips, he seemed to be saying: "You must be mad! And I do not get involved in stuff like that. A cockroach doesn't have any business in cock foul party."

It was then I called 911 on my iPhone. The police took forever to arrive. They were not even able to play catchup in pursuit of that SUV which by then had an enormous head-start on its getaway route. Detective Hobbs and Johnson on the scene documented her statement and corroborated it with Louise Dipson's profile.

THE N Y CONNIVERS SERIES

20

As was done before: after Dipson first struck in Williamsburg, roadblocks were once again set up. The Mt. Vernon police collaborated in the search for those missing girls. This time mostly along exit off and on-ramps. Traffic on the Major Deacon Expressway crawled heading north towards the Canadian border. Even though

THE N Y CONNIVERS SERIES

heading north for Dipson would put her at risk unless she exited before crossing the Canadian border.

There her vehicle would no doubt get searched and swept by Canadian border patrols. Mounted police were poised and armed just in case Dipson dared cross over into Canadian territory. The news of this NYC-based serial abductor had already saturated the CBC airwaves in Buffalo, New York, and across the border. Contrariwise, heading south could also be a risky proposition to make as the Bronx River Parkway, the George Washington Bridge heading into New Jersey, and the Henry Hudson Parkway heading into Manhattan's westside, were baited traps in waiting for this getaway SUV.

Law Enforcement was now getting into Dipson's psyche. As she cleverly navigated those side streets in upper New York. They were clever at determining how one of their own would think in all those given circumstances. Even so, Louise Dipson countered. Except once again she enticed them on a wild goose chase. They looked for her on the major streets. In the meantime, she rolled along the side streets. Dipson was never found so they once again found themselves sucking their thumbs. How they wished someone would say:

THE N Y CONNIVERS SERIES

"I saw something. A vehicle looking like Dipson's. Anything."

It was not a case wherein she was stationary. But she was clever enough to travel underneath their radar. Always one step ahead of any of their blueprints to catch her. Anything for them to go on. Victims number 8 and 9 abductees had already gotten stuck in her spider web and became deeply entangled. Now she was on a quest for more victims and desperately had to be stopped before she struck again.

Multiple scenarios bombarded the minds of Hobbs and Johnson. The chess game was on and Dipson focused on how to strategically move all her Kingmen every time they blinked. She knew as long as they didn't stop her, she held the upper hand. Already there were multiple questions with still limited answers. Some New Yorkers entertained: "The Internal Affairs should have gone easy on Dipson when she prostituted. Plus, getting pregnant was not only her right but it was her body and not someone else's."

No matter what analogy they used to describe her cop -cop-turned-teen-predator-persona. She was putting them to the test and not only using up their mental faculties and resources for her selfish benefit

THE N Y CONNIVERS SERIES

but predating on those innocent girls. Teens who had nothing to do with the death of her daughter, Cherae.

THE N Y CONNIVERS SERIES

21

For days it seemed as if the entire investigation was put on deep froze. Inside the department, the lead detectives Hobbs and Johnson gave the impression as if their hands were completely tied behind their backs. While displaying a total façade. They were now information-laden and ultimately result-empty. Even so, news continued circulating

THE N Y CONNIVERS SERIES

and spun out of control in the media. The predator could be lurking in your neighborhood. Freedom of the Press could be an investigative monster at times. They continually kept the public on high alert. While some complained law enforcement wasn't doing enough to solve these crimes and bring the predator to justice. The press stayed constant.

It was clear Dipson was not the average wannabe criminal. She was adept, a notch above the rest. According to her profile archived by NYPD, she was street smart, law enforcement savvy, and physically fit. Additionally, she knew how to get in and out of any situation and eventually trapped her pursuers while doing so. In short, going after this predator they realized they had their hands full.

On the other hand, most believed with all this beefed-up presence put in place by the Governor of New York, it could be just a matter of time before she plunged inside their baited net. However, to do so, these two detectives realized they had to bring their "A" game. They kept sorting bait. The water was warm, but their bait wasn't suitable for catching that fish.

Tick! Tick! The clock was ticking fast and young teen girls were more scared of the outdoors even when accompanied by an adult. Additionally, not only the police but parents and teachers were also on edge.

THE N Y CONNIVERS SERIES

They wanted the predator captured before she struck again. Not tomorrow, next week, next month or next year but now. One more parent in peril over the disappearance of their teen girl was more than NYC could manage. While these talking points festered. News broke that two park rangers saw a flock of vultures frequenting the woodlands of Westchester County. They followed their lead and subsequently discovered two bodies deep in the Westchester County woodlands. A location close to where the body of Cherae Dipson was found more than two years ago. Police helicopters were dispatched and soon circled overhead as these two brutally mutilated bodies of the last teens abducted at Dyre Avenue in the Bronx were airlifted in body-bags and out of that bereaved commune.

THE N Y CONNIVERS SERIES

22

With fingers continually pointing at Louise Dipson the predator. Law enforcement once again had it right. The bodies of those two teen girls bore the same resemblance of those previously abducted in the last two months and linked to Louise Dipson. Now bringing the sting of murders to nine.

THE N Y CONNIVERS SERIES

Neighbors in that Westchester community and residing close to the woodlands were particularly questioned. Yet, no one claimed they saw anything or encountered anyone driving a midnight blue SUV by day or night.

The lead detectives, Hobbs and Johnson were now more frantic than ever. Nothing they've done so far led them to catch this predator who kept leaving dead bodies behind a sign she was still active. It became apparent detectives were looking for a needle in a haystack or what some classified a wild goose chase. Consequently, they revisited Calderon in prison. Hobbs, before producing the idea to make this visit, decided he was going to press Calderon once again for answers. Hoping he would drop some bread crumbs. Johnson approved. Hobbs entertained the idea that if Calderon was somehow promised a light sentence, he might consider flipping. Thus, providing answers to assist in capturing Dipson.

They were cognizant of this one fact: In the past perpetrators indicted by the Southern District of New York court were apt to become rats in order to reduce their sentence. Aiding prosecutors to their ultimate target.

Hobbs, on this particular visit, was even willing to offer Calderon full immunity in order for him to fully cooperate as per the prosecutors. Yet, Calderon

THE N Y CONNIVERS SERIES

would not buy in. He preferred keeping his cards close to his chest. Calderon's defense liked what the detectives were offering his client. They felt this would eventually let him off the hook. To all this, he said:

"I cannot be a RAT. I would rather suffer the consequences. I'm an old man and could die soon, prison or no prison. So, with that said, I prefer to let sleeping dogs lie. It's water under the bridge as far as I can see it."

This frustrated the two detectives. Hobbs reached for his gun, stuck it inside Antonio Calderon's mouth as Calderon was in a "Ha hah. I'm not going to rattle on anyone. Put that in your pipe and smoke it – mode." Hobbs released the gun's safety threatening to waste Calderon.

"Who else was complicit in this serial spree, preying on young teens?"

Asked Hobbs.

Calderon gasped, he choked and stood up with bent knees. Hobbs stood up giving himself the necessary leverage to accommodate a direct deepthroated pallet removal.

"Sam…Saamy?"

Uncomfortably, asked Calderon.

"Sammy who?"

Asked the two detectives in touché mode.

THE N Y CONNIVERS SERIES

"Sammy Grant!"

Belched Calderon. At this stage, the Lieutenant walked in, and Hobbs released his draw. Now with a name to go on. Johnson winked at Hobbs; knowing they had a principal. They departed emboldened. However, the department stonewalled the information on Sammy Grant's whereabouts.

THE N Y CONNIVERS SERIES

23

Later that day. The FBI raided the home of Louise Dipson in Crown Heights. She was not there. However, they hauled away computers, boxes of documents and picture portraits. The following morning Louise Dipson struck yet again in an unrelated locale. This time outside a grocery store in the South Bronx.

THE N Y CONNIVERS SERIES

In broad daylight, yet another teen girl was abducted. An astute onlooker ventured in pursuit. However, he encountered problems as he tried starting up his pickup truck. When he finally got it started. An eighteen-wheeler had double-parked moments before and blocked his exit. The motorist blew his vehicle's horn constantly to no avail.

In the meantime, he dialed 911 on his iPhone. By the time the driver of the eighteen-wheeler returned to set him free from that parking spot, Detective Hobbs, and Johnson previously stationed at the Dyre Avenue subway station, bore down onto the scene in their unmarked sedan.

Instantly, additional Police vehicles swarmed the street like bees on a beehive. The now-relieved motorist points them north. They pursued hastily northbound as a convoy - raced.

For miles, they traveled like Alice in Wonderland. Suddenly as if miraculously, they caught up with that midnight blue mud-layered SUV pulling out of a gas station.

Now multiple car lengths ahead it left them in the dust. The number of police vehicles in the town increased. Johnson in the passenger seat of their sedan logged in its temporary license tags only to find the search came back - invalid.

THE N Y CONNIVERS SERIES

Already on high alert, instantaneous roadblocks created a detour instead of a flytrap. As if sensing their directives, the motorist in the SUV still oblivious to the pursuing lead detectives sensed their angle and orchestrated an individual diversion. The effects of this detour were only temporary.

The SUV ramped onto a two-lane highway leading away from the City's limits and through the woodlands. Police vehicle sirens crescendo as cops blazed ahead in pursuit. Overhead helicopters join the search. The two lead detectives in the front car of this convoy were now bearing down on this runaway SUV with guns drawn.

While thick shrubbery barred Aerial vision. Unpredictably, a slow-moving deer crossed the street in front of the lead sedan. The cruiser slammed into the animal and turned a 90-degree angle in the road. Meanwhile, this tailing vehicle slammed into its rear fender and those on each other's tail into their lead. Helicopter police notified of a multiple-car pile-up tried landing but aborted the mission due to insufficient wingspan accommodation and dense fog. With the chase curtailed in a vehicular pileup, officers assessed the damage and licked their wounds. As Hobbs regained his presence of mind he radioed in for assistance. It was relayed back via text:

THE N Y CONNIVERS SERIES

The name Sammy Grant loomed largely. Sammy's semen sample was found in and on all the girls who were abducted and murdered since Louise Dipson began to prowl.

Law enforcement had been staking out in front of Sammy's house in Crown Heights, Brooklyn using Crown Heights Security Patrol vehicles. Ironically, it seemed his house had no dwellers as delivered mail was hanging out of his mailbox.

It now became a sudden toss-up for Hobbs and Johnson. Continue going after Louise Dipson or concentrate on the bird in hand, Sammy Grant? The pursuit of Dipson ran cold while news of Sammy Grant simmered. Soon police helicopters circling overhead retreated.

The NYPD ended up slowing their roll in pursuit of Louise Dipson minutes later. She had already eluded them and vanished.

With the search now impaired as Dipson's getaway had occurred. Hobbs and Johnson followed their tip which led them to Crown Heights, Brooklyn on that Friday evening. The close-knit Jewish neighborhood with its own CHSP units, Ambulance fleet, and multiple street cameras. It was a planned off night for the CHSP.

Going undercover in an unmarked vehicle served the detectives well to not disturb the community on the

THE N Y CONNIVERS SERIES

eve of their sabbath. Every door for business is now closed except for the neighborhood Cleaners, barricades moved in place along Eastern Parkway and Kingston Avenue.

Sammy Grant's house is nestled among one of these establishments. It became a growing concern for the commune as the FBI had recently raided Louise Dipson's house in that same neighborhood, a few days prior. As the detectives pulled up. Grant was on his way out.

"How convenient!"

Hobbs whispered to Johnson. They made the calculated arrest and read to him his Miranda rights. Multiple unmarked police vehicles converged on Kingston Avenue and Eastern Parkway as Sammy was hauled away on Sabbath's eve.

THE N Y CONNIVERS SERIES

24

Before booking Sammy Grant on charges. The two lead detectives endeavored to get as much as they could out of him. He was more cooperative than Calderon. In that, he confessed he was complicit with Calderon in assaulting and raping those young girls. Additionally, he was tied

THE N Y CONNIVERS SERIES

to the string of abductions with Louise Dipson. It was becoming obvious Grant was leaning towards becoming an informant even without his legal counsel present.

While the news of Sammy Grant's arrest percolated in the media. Pimp Daddy's name became a high priority on the lead detective's list. Once the New York pimp's name dropped, they became busily connecting the dots.

On the other hand, Grant told the authorities he joined the team due to Pimp Daddy's solicitation. Grant provided in his statement that he became involved with the girls in conjunction with Pimp Daddy and Antonio Calderon. Grant even stated he paid Pimp Daddy to sleep with these girls. When asked if he later shared the girls with Calderon. He stated:

"Calderon was a man of enormous wealth and paid his way."

"Calderon was a business mogul in operation for most of his adult life."

Said Sammy Grant. The assortment of problems was now ajar in this investigative process. In other words: Drip by drip the giant rock was being unseated. When questioned concerning Dipson, Grant, however, remained tight-lipped.

"What was he hiding? Why was he trying to protect Dipson?"

The detectives queried during their lunch recess. When they returned and regrouped those questions were once again raised. Sammy Grant adeptly dogged the Dipson bullet.

"If Grant wanted immunity it was clear he had to come clean and give up all the necessary information relating to his crimes. Including any or all in complicit to Dipson."

Bolstered, Detective Johnson.

It was obvious that Dipson already spearheaded this operation and whatever it took to lead detectives to her before she struck again would be beneficial to the detectives in parceling their investigation. Yet, Grant about Dipson sat on everything Louise Dipson. Hobbs and Johnson were now busily going through Pimp Daddy's profile after Grant floated his name.

At one point, Pimp Daddy was the wealthiest pimp in NYC. No wonder Calderon aligned himself with the Pimp. Not only that, but he was also the father of Cherae Dipson, Louise's daughter.

As a result of his involvement with Louise Dipson while she worked for the NYPD, Louise was terminated from the department after an internal affairs investigation possibly influenced by her boss

THE N Y CONNIVERS SERIES

Captain Jerome Meeks. Nevertheless, Pimp Daddy still had her back.

THE N Y CONNIVERS SERIES

25

At daybreak, Hobbs and Johnson arrested Pimp Daddy in Westchester exiting a local bar. They tried to get whatever they could from Pimp Daddy in terms of a confession. He as in the case of Calderon remained tight-lipped. Their coverup was growing more teeth. A LOUISE

THE N Y CONNIVERS SERIES

DIPSON (THE detectives felt certain if they could get Pimp Daddy to eventually come clean, they could bring down Louise Dipson. Meanwhile, there was no information on the last girl who was abducted outside that Bronx Convenient Store. With Dipson still at large law enforcement remained on edge.

The attorneys representing Calderon in a Cable News interview claimed their client would be willing to clear his name. If given a chance to do so on TV. It was apparent that two of Calderon's associates were now indicted and incarcerated he could be in deep waters. That was good news as people glued to the case wanted to hear from this elderly man who kept his mouth shut. Even so, they remained optimistic he would be willing to move the needle in their investigation.

On the other hand, as if suffering from Alzheimer's, by the time Calderon's defense brought him to the pond he wouldn't drink. Life imprisonment or not. Causing TV anchors to wait in vain.

The prosecution felt as if Calderon, an adept gambler was taking them on a wild goose chase. One day he wanted to fess up. Then he chose not to say a word.

In a conversation between Hobbs and Johnson off the record Hobbs told Johnson:

"When it comes to Calderon's statement, we are going to have to get to Dipson even without his help.

THE N Y CONNIVERS SERIES

Too bad Sammy Grant wouldn't give us a window when LOUISE DIPSON comes to Louise Dipson. What a freaking unadulterated cover-up!"

THE N Y CONNIVERS SERIES

26

While the news of Sammy Grant and Pimp Daddy's arrest reached Louise Dipson. She had just completed masking herself and heading out to capture her next victim. Walking out of her hotel room she looked at her most recent victim twisting in pain and tied up with ropes to the

THE N Y CONNIVERS SERIES

bed frame. She was eventually stung with a change of heart.

Shaking her head, Louise Dipson closed the door to her hotel room and departed. Up the street and several blocks away she boarded that midnight blue SUV and departed. Purposed in her mind it was time to do it solo.

Louise was well known for exerting her independence. Even without Pimp Daddy in the picture. She felt she had this.

Immediately, she tapped into that vein, and instead of calling the police and surrendering she drove herself to the police station, parked the SUV in the parking lot, threw the keys on the passenger seat, locked the abduction mobile, walked away, and entered the Bronx Police Station.

Multiple police officers met her at the door in takedown style. Not that they were expecting her, but they saw in their surveillance video when the SUV pulled up and made sure even their desk officers were fully armed for combat.

Dipson casually put her hands over her head at their command. They rushed in, frisked her, and administered handcuffs. As the news spread. It surprised most law enforcement that Louise Dipson turned herself in. After running for weeks unleashed. However, with her accomplices now behind bars.

THE N Y CONNIVERS SERIES

They felt she was subordinated and wearied. According to Hobbs:

"Dipson had no choice but to give herself up to us. She is tired of playing the cat-and-mouse game. Now she has been declawed…"

THE N Y CONNIVERS SERIES

27

The news disseminated exponentially. "Louise Dipson the predator gave herself up to law enforcement in the Bronx." "The fast-food business is now operating full throttle." Expressed one Vegan enthusiast showing off a celery stick. Parents, teens, churches, schools, as well as other

THE N Y CONNIVERS SERIES

teen-related institutions, were now all rendering PRAISE for what
had transpired. She was finally off the streets. Now they were free to conduct business as usual.
On the other hand, some remained skeptical that Dipson might still be at large. They watched the news over and over again for comfort in the fact she had ceased and desist. Some even called the NYPD to ensure Dipson was securely behind bars.
The facts bore out. It was corroborated by the Governor's office: The Predator had cooled her heels. Now they were free to conduct business as usual. It is said:
"With every new level, there's a new Devil."
That truism bore fruit as now law enforcement's new problem dangled as they focused on potential copycats. "What if others replicated her actions?" They whined. After coming to grips. They realized Louise Dipson engaged in a vendetta.
See, after Dipson's surrender to law enforcement, they realized she was partly acting out of revenge for her daughter Cherae's death. As was mentioned, the girl's body was recovered from the woodlands in Westchester County, raped, and brutally mutilated. Whoever conducted those brutal acts was still a mystery.

THE N Y CONNIVERS SERIES

On the other hand, it was determined if Sammy Grant would truly cooperate. Those charges against him LOUISE DIPSON (THE PREDATOR) 94 94 could disintegrate. It seemed he was prepared to tease law enforcement with one foot in and one foot out. That talking point simmered in the media as well as the legal arena for days. Now like a popcorn effect, more evidence in the case popped up.

Now, DNA tests linked Sammy Grant to the rape of Cherae Dipson. It was determined that the semen specimen found at the crime scene of the young Dipson as well as multiple other sexual assault victims matched Sammy Grant's DNA.

So, even though Grant felt warm in the prosecutors' pocket. Those cold winds of two years ago had returned like a Northeaster to chill his butt.

On the other hand, Dipson was fighting with those tentacles of surrender. She refused to provide information leading to the whereabouts of her last victim. As she wavered through the night. In the wee hours of the morning, a hotel housekeeper at the Bronx Hotel discovered the victim Nikia Chavez tied to the bed frame of the hotel's bed frame.

THE N Y CONNIVERS SERIES

28

As the Breaking News in this convoluted Dipson episodic spread. Pimp Daddy and Louise Dipson, now on bail, collectively filed a lawsuit against Sammy Grant for the unlawful death of their daughter Cherae Dipson. The rumor became widespread; Pimp Daddy could have

THE N Y CONNIVERS SERIES

obliviously been the one responsible for bringing Sammy Grant on board this killing spree on the behest of Louise Dipson. It was also widespread: Calderon and Grant both paid hefty sums for their involvement with those teen girls and were regarded as pedophiles.

Once again Hobbs and Johnson went back to the drawing board and quizzed Calderon to see if he was ready to spill more beans. Anything about his collaboration with Grant at this point could set this investigation into overdrive they reckoned. However, Calderon once again remained mute.

On the other hand, Grant, when asked about his involvement in the rape and murder of Cherae Dipson, he resorted to pleading the fifth on that matter. Thus, leaving the prosecution stuck with a contaminated witness – himself.

As if miraculously, the lawsuit against Sammy Grant superseded the Louise Dipson and company trial in SDNY.

There erupted a keen sense of public sentiment for the suit brought against Sammy Grant by Louise Dipson and Pimp Daddy. Ironically, the defense team of Samuel Taliaferro and Calista Cochran was retained, and a court date was set at SDNY.

Dipson and Pimp Daddy very much liked the odds delivered in the previous Brad versus Beverly Tyson

THE N Y CONNIVERS SERIES

– LOUISE DIPSON (THE PREDATOR) 97 97 Smith case in which Brad Smith was acquitted. To them, Taliaferro was their hometown hero, and Cochran their Big Apple heroine.

THE N Y CONNIVERS SERIES

29

The first day of this lawsuit Louise Dipson and Pimp Daddy versus Sammy Grant captured the media's attention. Outside on the steps leading to inside the courthouse the lectern, littered with media microphones waited. Louise Dipson

THE N Y CONNIVERS SERIES

walked up to the microphones wearing GPS ankle bracelets. Claiming she could have been set up.
"By whom?"
One reporter asked.
"You know who."
Replied Louise Dipson.
At this point, her layer Samuel Taliaferro interceded: "This is a case in which we're seeking justice for the murder of the young teen Cherae Dipson. After two years, we are happy to be positioned to move this case forward."
That's all the news media got as they were left hanging for more. However, they took what they got and ran with it. She was mute when she turned herself in to law enforcement. Plus, she has been quiet in public since. In this opportunity at the lectern that's all she wrote, and they expediently published it.
Spinning it in many directions as they could. Compounded with the talking point that the community of Crown Heights was torn. Jewish neighbors of the Dipsons' joined in a community demonstration and pleaded for a conviction of Sammy Grant also from their neighborhood.
On the one hand, they nurtured a teen killer in Sammy Grant. Many now saw his residence as a sore eye in the Crown Heights community. Sammy Grant

THE N Y CONNIVERS SERIES

had not only raped and murdered one of their teen idols, but he was alleged to be complicit in the rape and death of nine other young teen girls.

THE N Y CONNIVERS SERIES

30

Opening arguments swiftly began inside the courtroom at SDNY. The prosecution argued that Sammy Grant, a known murderer now sentenced to 20 years to be served in Attica, New York for the killing of Cherae Dipson. He previously hitched himself to the wagon of Pimp

THE N Y CONNIVERS SERIES

Daddy, Calderon, and Louise Dipson, enabling him to continue his killing spree. This event stemmed from over two years ago with Cherae Dipson.

During the cross-examination of Pimp Daddy, it was revealed that Louise Dipson who retained the right not to testify, was coerced into the seriality of young teen girls by defendant Sammy Grant.

On the other hand, it was revealed that Sammy Grant and Calderon funded the operation. The prosecutors tried hard not to mix the two cases involving Grant's criminality.

Even so, it was not easy as Grant's criminal activities were already baked into the cake. It had become obvious that Sammy Grant was adept at what he did. At the time, he joined the Louise Dipson team and, in some ways, spearheaded her criminal operation. Both Louise Dipson and Pimp Daddy were not aware Grant was solely responsible for the killing of their daughter Cherae Dipson at the time he joined their squad.

Pimp Daddy was asked by the defense:

"If you had the chance to do it all over again, what would be his strategy?"

To which he responded.

"I've never wanted to roll that way, but with the promptings of Sammy Grant and his skill set, it became apparent we could work together, not

THE N Y CONNIVERS SERIES

knowing much of his criminal past. Wished I knew before he murdered our daughter."

THE N Y CONNIVERS SERIES

31

Sammy Grant, on the other hand, claimed he had nothing to do with the death of Cherae Dipson. Even though Grant's DNA placed him fairly and squarely not only at the murder scene but as a sexual connection. It was clear Sammy Grant anticipated he would get away with this two-year-old murder of the young Dipson, which came back to

THE N Y CONNIVERS SERIES

haunt him. He evidently flew under the radar for some time as law enforcement was unable to nab him as the brutal murderer in that murder case.

Sammy Grant knowingly joined forces with Pimp Daddy, Calderon, and Louise Dipson.

" Sammy Grant enlisted himself as the catalyst."

Said Pimp Daddy. "He was a prizefighter and very good in the ring. A man who can land a punch so hard his opponent would fall immediately to the ground." Said a Sports Reporter who also claimed: " As a fighter, Sammy Grant emulated the fighting tactics of the Heavy Weight Boxer – Mike Tyson."

It was also discovered that those victims who bore evidence of the brutality traced to those concussions were inflicted by someone with – Sammy Grant's sized hands.

Louise Dipson, sitting inside that courtroom broke down in tears as the pictures of the murder scene where Cherae's body was discovered, screen-slide and introduce again in this duplicitous murder saga. She made the sign of the cross on multiple occasions. Pimp Daddy realized how deeply involved Louise Dipson was in the criminal enterprise and a non-testifying witness, so he took the brunt of the beating from Grant's defense. They labeled Pimp Daddy not only as an accomplice in the murder of those teen girls but as a pimp he decided he would not get off

the trail. So, he downscaled his operation. Instead, he decided to prey on young girls.

Pimp Daddy's distance from the new string of seriality for which he was indicted hung over his head like a thick cloud and even rained inside the courtroom as Louise Dipson teared up some more.

THE N Y CONNIVERS SERIES

32

Meanwhile, Sammy Grant at one point, endeavored to cast blame. pointed fingers at both Pimp Daddy and Louise Dipson as the possible killers of their daughter Cherae. Some claimed he had three fingers pointing back at him. Additionally, Grant claimed during a conversation with Pimp Daddy, the infamous NYC Pimp

disclosed he liked young girls. Mainly around the ages of 14 – 17. The prosecution argued that there was no meat in that statement, seeing it was just hearsay. However, in this decade, the talking point was relevant, seeing one of the infamous young teen girl sexual offenders was recently incarcerated and subsequently committed suicide while incarcerated.

Also, Sammy Grant alluded to Pimp Daddy being intoxicated constantly. Therefore, he could have been an incest participant in his daughter's death.

That anecdote was ludicrous in the eyes of the jury as frowns were detected on some faces. Even so, Grant was willing to push the lid on this supposition. He further stated:

"When it comes down to sexual assault, he wouldn't put anything past Pimp Daddy due to his tenure as a notorious pimp."

Once again, all of this smelled like a smoking gun but without any fire.

The jury of 12 returned a guilty verdict in this lawsuit against Sammy Grant. However, it was discovered that Sammy Grant was out of money. In other words, he looked good and smelled good but was physically flat broke. According to sources managing his depleted finances, the only asset to his name was that brownstone home he owned in Crown Heights.

THE N Y CONNIVERS SERIES

Additionally, during his sentencing, he received 20 years in prison for the murder of Cherae Dipson. Her parents were awarded his $750.000.00 Brownstone in Crown Heights in the lawsuit. However, still on the docket in SDNY, the trial in which Grant was also indicted for participating in the killing of 9 other young teen girls in New York.

THE N Y CONNIVERS SERIES

33

While jurors were being selected in the upcoming Louise Dipson the Predator, Pimp Daddy, Sammy Grant, and Calderon versus the Government trial. Many legal scholars, as well as the media, very much anticipated the testimony

of Nikia Gomez the lone survivor in this abduction spree. It was widespread among some of her peers. Nikia got what she deserved. Mainly because she spent time together with the wrong crowd.

Previously, Nikia lived in Crown Heights, Brooklyn, and attended CHH. Moving to the Bronx she underwent a complete makeover. Nikia not only changed her hairstyle but added multiple nose rings and tattoos. Nothing about her resembled the Nikia of Crown Heights.

Living in the Bronx, she was known to have defied just about every curfew issued by her adoptive parents. It was reported that her parents were summoned to a parent-teacher meeting after a crack-pipe was discovered inside her locker. To which Nikia claimed she didn't know how it got there.

Additionally, some of those same peers had reported her drug dilemma not only to other students but to teachers and principals as well. In that school, Nikia was categorized as a basket case. However, she was the sole victim out of all the alleged abductees conducted by Dipson still alive.

During Nikia's testimony, the prosecution armed themselves with as much evidence as they possibly could. Their objective, even though Louise Dipson

had lost her daughter Cherae Dipson, murdered by Sammy Grant, they not only wanted to see Louise Dipson rot in prison but possibly fry in the electric chair.

The media in the intervening time, did an entire spin on the trial, stating Dipson was guilty of all these crimes even before any witnesses were introduced in this trial.

Additionally, Nikia in her statement to Detective Hobbs and Johnson, claimed she was previously raped by Sammy Grant and that he threatened to do it again if she did not cooperate sexually. This was said to her a day before Louise Dipson turned herself in.

The forensic DNA evidence also linked Sammy Grant to Nikia. She claimed Grant conducted her abduction by throwing a bag over her head. Coincidentally, Nikia in a statement to the detectives said: She eluded innuendos made by Sammy Grant while she attended CHH as he frequented the neighborhood's post office across from the school. She broke down talking about guarding Cherae on the basketball court.

The prosecutor opined Nikia would administer the keypunch in the trial and was poised for the trial to get underway. While New York's toughest maximum security prison waited with outstretched

THE N Y CONNIVERS SERIES

tentacles for the criminals involved in the serial enterprise.

THE N Y CONNIVERS SERIES

34

The trial eventually began and after opening arguments, the prosecution brought the infamous detectives Johnson followed by Hobbs to the stand. Detective Johnson claimed she and her partner were first called to the McDonald's parking lot in Williamsburg. It was in response to a

THE N Y CONNIVERS SERIES

911 call regarding the abduction of two teen girls – Deslyn Soprano and Maddy St. Hilaire.
She stated upon arrival, the parking lot was practically filled with neighbors, friends, and the two sets of discombobulated parents.
"They never got into any trouble."
Claimed Deslyn Soprano's parents approaching before we could get out of our cruiser.
Meanwhile, the manager of that McDonald's, Angie Gomez headed in our direction upset. We accommodated Gomez's statement in a separate huddle. She told us:
"The girls looked like they were about fourteen. They made their purchase and instead of eating in they opt to head outside."
She gushed.
 "Suddenly, as if by a flash of lightning a midnight-blue SUV pulled up, the girls were rushed inside on the rear seat, and it took off speedily heading eastbound." She continued.
We have been continually in investigative mode of Louise Dipson, since. Later we arrested Antonio Calderon an accomplice of the perpetrator Louise Dipson. Our investigation also helped us to bring down other accomplices, Pimp Daddy, and Sammy Grant.

THE N Y CONNIVERS SERIES

Nine young teen girls were found murdered as a result of this alleged abduction serial spree.

Our first real encounter with Dipson began in a chase through Westchester County aborted in a road-kill accident. Louise Dipson eluded us, after a multiple police car pile-up. Days later she turned herself in at our South Bronx precinct."

Her partner Jonathan Hobbs corroborated her testimony.

THE N Y CONNIVERS SERIES

35

As the trial continued; the McDonald's manager Arlene Gomez was put on the stand. During her cross-examination, the defense questioned: Gomez was sure at that time of the evening and almost dark?

"How did you recognize the color of the getaway vehicle? It could have been black or dark gray." To which Arlene Gomez responded:

THE N Y CONNIVERS SERIES

"I know my colors. It was not black or gray. It was midnight blue. Here's a picture of the curb in the driveway that her vehicle grazed while she speedily tried to get away."

The picture was entered into evidence after matching up with an indentation on the SUV's photographic experiment.

Additionally, the experiment of the SUV was put up on the screen. Gomez assured the jury and the entire court that the vehicle in question was the getaway SUV.

The prosecution seemed as though they were in a rush to close the case. Weeping parents inside that SDNY courtroom anticipated a speedy climax. Pressure from the media, as well as those bereaved, was like a weight on the prosecution's back.

Additionally, Senators, Congressmen, and other government officials were all applying pressure toward a swift verdict. It was like a stain on the judicial system as well as NYC. Most of those New York senator's seats remained vulnerable as the upcoming election was speedily approaching. Law enforcement was blamed for not doing enough to solve crime in the big city.

On the other hand, the prosecution could have called Sammy Grant to testify at this point and fulfilled the wish of the bereaved. Instead, they called Nikia

THE N Y CONNIVERS SERIES

Chavez the lone surviving victim. Nikia detailed she was about to visit the convenience store to buy groceries for her mother.

"The SUV pulled up as she crossed the street to enter. Louise Dipson was in the driver's seat. The rear door opened automatically.

Sammy Grant jumped out from the back seat. He put a bag over my head, one hand over my mouth, put my arm in a clinch behind my back, and shoved me inside that SUV. He jumped in behind me. The door closed of its own accord and the thing drove off speedily. It seems like he was after me for years. I remembered him winking at me whenever our paths crossed at the local Post Office.

THE N Y CONNIVERS SERIES

36

Inside the courtroom. You can hear a pin drop. Heads turned. "What happened then?" Asked Claudia Mendez for the prosecution.

"The SUV drove through the city streets and into some deserted areas. Grant kept touching me in private areas. Asked me if I was a virgin. I told him I

was. He told me he's a master at lovemaking. At this point, I felt cold sweats all over my body."
"What was the driver Louise Dipson doing at this point?"
Asked Mendez.
"She turned up the music loudly and continued speeding like a maniac."
Said Nikia.
"What else did Sammy Grant do?"
"He kept blowing into my left ear. I kept on resisting his advance. He asked me why I was trying to be a Little B... I told him I had a boyfriend."
"Tell me more. What else?"
Asked Prosecutor Mendez. Louise Dipson pulled up on a side street filled with high shrubbery. She parked the SUV and attempted to get out. I yelled: Please don't do this to me! She proceeded anyway and slammed the door shut. He continued fondling me, removed my outer layers of clothing, and raped me. He repeated himself multiple times: You were not a good girl and I'll give you a chance to redeem yourself tomorrow." "What else?"
"He stuck an inhaler up my nose. That's the last thing I remembered."
"So, how did you wind up at the hotel?"
Asked Mendez.
Nikia broke down in tears.

THE N Y CONNIVERS SERIES

"Not sure."
Said Nikia. "
When I woke up. I found myself tied up with rope to the bedframe in the hotel room."
Continued Nikia. Did you know or ever met Cherae's mom Louise Dipson when you lived in Brooklyn and attended Crown Heights High?"
"Never did. But Cherry always bragged about her mother. Saying she's a born leader who's unstoppable and pushes her to succeed at astronomical levels." "You mean Cherae."
"Yes. My friends and I called her Cherry because she dripped sweetness. Always such a giving person."
"What was she like on the court?"
Asked Claudia Mendez.
"Cherry was almost ungradable. She was our team's idol. Also, the idol of Crown Heights."
Says Nikia.
"Do you despise Sammy Grant now that you learned he was convicted and sentenced for taking Cherae Dipson's life?"
Asked the prosecution.
"You bet! I hate him!"
Responds Nikia. She teared up once again. So, did her mother sit in that courtroom?
Multiple jurors seemed locked into her story evident by their body language. Meanwhile, Louise Dipson

remained poker-faced. The Teen Advocate from the Williamsburg crime scene was seen taking copious notes inside that courtroom. Once again Nikia welled up in tears and had to be aided off the witness stand and back to her seat. Judge Thomas tactfully ordered a court recess. Which eventually materialized into a court adjournment until the next day.

THE N Y CONNIVERS SERIES

37

The media went on a continued tirade overnight infused with talking points from Nikia Chavez's testimony. Early in the morning, the defense began their cross of Nikia Chavez. They came at her with everything they could benefit their client Sammy Grant.

THE N Y CONNIVERS SERIES

Everything from that crack pipe found in her locker at school was thrown at her testimony. They labeled her as a crackpot and a blatant liar. Even asserting her trip to the grocery store could have been for the purchase of narc. That locale was later closed down by the Feds after a raid in which a huge volume of crack cocaine was seized.

"Why were you hanging out on that street?" Questioned the defense. They even argued and doubted Nikia ever encountered Sammy Grant prior and even labeled her as a gold digger. Nikia stuck to her testimony in an attempt to fend them off. Meanwhile, her mother in that courtroom could not stop her tear-flow.

Sammy Grant's defense questioned Louise Dipson's attitude throughout this abduction. Trying to nail her to the cross intended for Sammy Grant. Nikia once again gave those vivid details of her abduction and rape as previously presented in her testimony to the prosecution.

Louise Dipson sitting in that courtroom yelled: "Lying Bastard!"

While Taliaferro cross-examined Nika Chavez.

The judge cautioned Dipson with a penalty for disrupting the court proceedings.

THE N Y CONNIVERS SERIES

"Miss Dipson, if you are not willing to testify in your defense. I suggest you keep your comments to yourself. You can't have it both ways."

Dipson, in turn, held back her follow-up comment but later dropped under her breath. " Lying Bastards!" In the meantime, most of the jury engaged in taking copious notes.

The defense pressed the teenager Nikia Chavez but was unable to punch any holes into her testimony. Leaving the prosecution team of Douglas Tibbs and Claudia Mendez in a feel-good situation regarding the testimony of their star witness.

THE N Y CONNIVERS SERIES

38

Courtroom attendees by this time anticipated hearing from Pimp Daddy, Calderon, Sammy Grant, and of course, Louise Dipson if she was going to testify. The defense, knowing Taliaferro and Cochran could very much opt out of putting Dipson on the stand. While those thoughts

THE N Y CONNIVERS SERIES

simmered, the Judge called Pimp Daddy to the stand. Pimp Daddy took the oath. Feeling fresh from his testimony in the lawsuit against Sammy Grant.

Now like Déjà Vu, both men implicated in this series of crimes orchestrated by Louise Dipson were back in the same courtroom together. Both stared each other down nefariously.

Sammy Grant already sentenced in the first case in which he raped and brutally murdered the daughter of Louise Dipson and Pimp Daddy still showed remorse. As most expected and debated, Pimp Daddy pleaded the fifth in this Louise Dipson trial. He no doubt wanted to remain loyal to Louise Dipson and refrained from implicating her. So, after taking the oath he torpedoed into that fifth dimension.

Will we hear from Calderon or not? This double-faced question not only sucked up the air in the courtroom but also the media. A man senior in years and possessing enormous wealth would have much to say even though he previously pleaded the fifth. It seemed he wanted to walk back his decision to remain silent. His cold feet stepped in. He felt it was way too much for him, as he shook nervously in his shoes inside the courtroom. Antonio Calderon eventually folded and returned to his seat. Leaving

THE N Y CONNIVERS SERIES

the impression that it would take a crowbar to shake and lose whatever evidence he had in storage.

Next Sammy Grant was put on the hot seat. Getting a lighter sentence was foremost on his mind. He testified that he went along with the enterprise of Dipson, Calderon, and Pimp Daddy just for the ride. As if the person who drives the getaway car is not complicit in the robbery.

Nikia Chavez had already pointed fingers at Sammy Grant as her abductor, who, raped and also threatened her life. It was apparent the quicksand was swaying quickly; Sammy Grant had no way of getting out of this swamp.

Ironically, his defense put up a strong case. Reasoning his client wanted nothing to do with the string of concentrated murders. However, he was dragged into it by Calderon, Dipson and Pimp Daddy.

The prosecution argued he was adept at what he did and when the opportunity presented itself again, he preyed on those innocent teen girls. He no doubt had to prove to himself and the world at large that he could engage in this kind of conduct and get away with it. If he didn't want to be part of the ride why did he get on board?

THE N Y CONNIVERS SERIES

39

In Dipson's defense, Samuel Taliaferro pointed out that there was no evidence pointing her to the crime. Even the midnight-blue SUV was registered to Calderon along with that mint-green Land Rover. Plus, there was no DNA from Louise Dipson connected to any of the murdered victims.

THE N Y CONNIVERS SERIES

The only connection was to Nikia Chavez found on the ropes which were used to bind her.

The defense argued it was all hearsay. No one caught Dipson red-handed in any criminal activity. He also claimed his client was set up.

Additionally, when she saw how much damage Sammy Grant was causing to these young girls. She tied Nikia to the bedframe so Sammy Grant would not murder her in the woodlands. After which she turned herself in. He also argued: that Louise Dipson was never caught in the act and should not bear the penalty for someone else's crime.

On the other hand, the prosecution envisioned the maximum for Louise Dipson in this criminal conspiracy. Labeling her as the predator proves she is at the center of the operation.

"Her hands were dirty."

Said Claudia Mendez.

Also, the prosecution argued: that Louise Dipson because of her termination from the department became bitter and created a vendetta that she harbored and would do anything to harm the NYPD. By taking them on a wild goose chase and exploiting their resources.

Louise Dipson led a street life and no doubt passed some of her street life down to her daughter Cherae. So, to drag the NYPD on the brink of sabotage and

THE N Y CONNIVERS SERIES

catastrophe she illegally wore their uniform to commit acts of murder against these innocent young teen girls. Using taxpayers' money to set up roadblocks all over NYC to track her down.

THE N Y CONNIVERS SERIES

40

Sammy Grant, on the other hand, saw profit and pleasure in her enterprise and bought in, lock, stock, and barrel. Bringing Calderon along for support. In this, Calderon saw the opportunity to scar these young girls and collectively they exploited these 10 young teen girls.

THE N Y CONNIVERS SERIES

Pimp Daddy, settled in his enterprising ways could not keep his hand out of the till. Wherever he saw greed and profit he latched on as his extended way of life. Louise Dipson, Sammy Grant, Calderon, and Pimp Daddy deserve the maximum penalty allowed in New York State for their crimes. The jury would be doing less than they are capable of and shirking their civic duty if they didn't find them guilty as charged.

The defense for Calderon and Sammy Grant argued their clients were coerced by Dipson and Pimp Daddy, and that they should be acquitted or given much lighter sentences for their crimes.

Meanwhile, Taliaferro and Cochran tried to create sunlight between Antonio Calderon and Sammy Grant. They argued: that Louise Dipson didn't have the heart to commit those murders. Despite everything, she had gone through. As a mother, no wonder she turned herself in, instead of inflicting any harm on Nikia Chavez. There comes a point in everyone's life when they must decide: If not me. Who? If not now, When? This ultimately happened for Louise Dipson. That's why she stood up for her daughter even after a two-year-old murder. I feel she could someday become a champion of reform. She has already begun the process in that direction.

THE N Y CONNIVERS SERIES

After closing arguments, Judge Claude Thomas gaveled and sent the Jury to deliberate.

THE N Y CONNIVERS SERIES

41

While the trial was underway. Louise Dipson and Pimp Daddy had been covertly attending Bible studies at a local church. The point came when they resolved to give their lives to Jesus Christ. However, the Pastor informed them that to get baptized it's a prerequisite for them to tie the knot.

THE N Y CONNIVERS SERIES

Pimp Daddy was reluctant in getting married even if they had been together for years. Anyway, on a rainy Wednesday night in April, they were married in that neighborhood church. Witnesses to the event were Captain Jerome Meeks and Nicole Best-Meeks both recently married, and members of that church assembly. It turned into a double event as the couple was baptized thereafter.

The jury deliberated for twelve days and finally returned verdicts:

Sammy Grant was found guilty of rape, aiding, and abetting in a child abduction spree, and murdering seven young girls.

Calderon was found guilty of rape, aiding, and abetting in a child abduction spree.

Pimp Daddy was found guilty of aiding and abetting in a child abduction spree.

Louise Dipson was found guilty of the attempted murder of Nikia Chavez and aiding and abetting in a child abduction spree.

All four defendants in this enterprise are awaiting sentencing in SDNY. Each crime committed was expected to carry a penalty of at least 15 years or more in prison.

THE N Y CONNIVERS SERIES

THE N Y CONNIVERS SERIES

The Pullout

While this literary siege was underway which almost crippled NYC, a Cable TV Station rolled out the following insert:

At 2:35 on the afternoon of October 27, 1904, New York City Mayor George McClellan took control of the inaugural run of the city's innovative new rapid transit system: the subway.

While London boasts the world's oldest underground train network (opened in 1863) and Boston built the first subway in the United States in 1897, the New York City subway soon became the largest American system. The first line, operated by the Interborough Rapid Transit Company (IRT), traveled 9.1 miles through 28 stations. Running from City Hall in lower Manhattan to Grand Central Terminal in midtown, and then heading west along 42nd Street to Times Square, the line finished by zipping north, all the way to 145th Street and Broadway in Harlem. On opening day, Mayor McClellan so enjoyed his stint as an engineer that he stayed at the controls from City Hall to 103rd Street.

At 7 p.m. that evening, the subway opened to the general public, and more than 100,000 people paid a nickel each to take their first ride under Manhattan. IRT service expanded to the Bronx in 1905, to Brooklyn in 1908, and to Queens in 1915. Since 1968, the subway has been controlled by the Metropolitan Transport Authority (MTA). The system now has 26 lines and 468 stations in operation; the longest line, the 8th Avenue "A" Express train, stretches more than 32 miles, from the northern tip of Manhattan to the far southeast corner of Queens.

THE N Y CONNIVERS SERIES

Every day, at least 4.5 million passengers take the subway in New York. Except for the PATH train connecting New York with New Jersey and some parts of Chicago's elevated train system, New York's subway is the only rapid transit system in the world that runs 24 hours a day, seven days a week. No matter how crowded or dirty, the subway is one New York City institution few New Yorkers — or tourists — could not do without.

The New York City Subway is a rapid transit system that serves four of the five boroughs of New York City, New York: the Bronx, Brooklyn, Manhattan, and Queens. Its operator is the New York City Transit Authority (NYCTA), which is controlled by the Metropolitan Transportation Authority (MTA) of New York. In 2016, an average of 5.66 million passengers used the system daily, making it the busiest rapid transit system in the United States and the seventh busiest in the world.

The first underground line opened on October 27,

1904, almost 35 years after the opening of the first elevated line in New York City, which became the IRT Ninth Avenue Line. By the time the first subway opened, the lines had been consolidated into two privately owned systems, the Brooklyn Rapid Transit Company (BRT, later Brooklyn–Manhattan Transit Corporation, BMT) and the Interborough Rapid Transit Company (IRT). After 1913, all lines built for the IRT and most lines for the BRT were built by the city and leased to the companies. The first line of the city-owned and operated Independent Subway System (IND) opened in 1932; this system was intended to compete with the private systems and allow some of the elevated railways to be torn down. However, it was kept within the core of the city because of the low amount

THE N Y CONNIVERS SERIES

of startup capital provided to the municipal Board of Transportation by the state. This required it to be run "at cost", necessitating fares up to double the five-cent fare popular at the time.

Yes. The first subway cost five cents to ride: Annoyed about the impending fare hike? New Yorkers were pretty pissed when the original subway fare doubled from 5 to 10 cents. Brass tokens were introduced when fares were raised to 15 cents, as they couldn't construct turnstiles that would accept two different coins. Tokens -- once an icon of the NYC subway -- were used for fifty years before the MetroCard was introduced in 2003. There are 60 million tokens left over.

It took almost 10 years to eliminate tokens, and when they were finally discontinued in 2003, the MTA was left with 60 million tokens. After a few calls to the MTA, it seems what happened to them is still largely a mystery.

Back in 1940, the city took over running the previously privately operated systems. Some elevated lines closed immediately while others closed soon after. Integration was slow, but several connections were built between the IND and BMT, which now operate as one division called the B

Division. Since the IRT infrastructure is too small for B Division cars, the IRT remains its division, the A Division.

The NYCTA, a public authority presided over by New York City, was created in 1953 to take over the subway, bus, and streetcar operations from the city. The NYCTA was under the control of the state-level MTA in 1968. Soon after the MTA took control of the subway, New York City entered a fiscal crisis. It closed many elevated subway lines that became too expensive to maintain. Graffiti and crime became common, and

THE N Y CONNIVERS SERIES

equipment and stations fell into decrepit condition. The New York City Subway tried to stay solvent, so it had to make many service cutbacks and defer necessary maintenance projects. In the 1980s an $18 billion financing program for the rehabilitation of the subway began.

The September 11 attacks resulted in service disruptions, particularly on the IRT Broadway–Seventh Avenue Line, which ran directly underneath the World Trade Center. Sections of the tunnel, as well as the Cortlandt Street station, which was directly underneath the Twin Towers, were severely damaged and had to be rebuilt, requiring suspension of service on that line south of Chambers Street. Ten other nearby stations were temporarily closed. By March 2002, seven of those stations had reopened. The rest (except for Cortlandt Street on the IRT Broadway–Seventh Avenue Line) reopened on September 15, 2002, along with service south of Chambers Street.

Since the 2000s, expansions include the 7 Subway Extension that opened in September 2015, and the Second Avenue Subway, the first phase of which opened on January 1, 2017. However, at the same time, under-investment in the subway system led to a transit crisis that peaked in 2017.

Since its opening in 1904, in addition to the effects of Hurricane Sandy in 2014, this is by far the most crippling tragedy imaginarily to ever hit the NYC Subway System. Not only crippling the city but could have long-lasting effects.

THE N Y CONNIVERS SERIES

NEW YORK CITY BLUES

TABLE OF CONTENTS

```
THE PULLOUT....................................................284
CHAPTER ONE...................................................289
CHAPTER TWO...................................................293
CHAPTER THREE.................................................296
CHAPTER FOUR..................................................299
CHAPTER FIVE..................................................302
CHAPTER SIX...................................................306
CHAPTER SEVEN.................................................309
CHAPTER EIGHT.................................................313
CHAPTER NINE..................................................318
CHAPTER TEN...................................................323
CHAPTER ELEVEN................................................329
CHAPTER TWELVE................................................334
CHAPTER THIRTEEN..............................................340
CHAPTER FOURTEEN..............................................344
CHAPTER FIFTEEN...............................................347
CHAPTER SIXTEEN...............................................350
CHAPTER SEVENTEEN.............................................353
CHAPTER EIGHTEEN..............................................357
CHAPTER NINETEEN..............................................360
CHAPTER TWENTY................................................364
CHAPTER TWENTY ONE............................................367
CHAPTER TWENTY TWO............................................370
CHAPTER TWENTY THREE..........................................373
CHAPTER TWENTY FOUR...........................................376
CHAPTER TWENTY FIVE...........................................379
CHAPTER TWENTY SIX............................................382
CHAPTER TWENTY SEVEN..........................................384
CHAPTER TWENTY EIGHT..........................................388
CHAPTER TWENTY NINE...........................................391
CHAPTER THIRTY................................................396
CHAPTER THIRTY ONE............................................399
CHAPTER THIRTY TWO............................................402
CHAPTER THIRTY THREE..........................................406
CHAPTER THIRTY FOUR...........................................408
```

THE N Y CONNIVERS SERIES

1

G ridlock traffic dominates through midtown Manhattan. At Broadway Avenue and 34th Street, this flowing stream of traffic becomes static. To put it bluntly, it resembles a parking lot. It eases up momentarily. Yellow cabs aggressively pick up the hastened but deposit them shortly thereafter. They exit disgustingly, slamming taxi doors shut, and opt to tread their distance on foot instead.

THE N Y CONNIVERS SERIES

Meanwhile, frustrated pedestrians vent as law enforcement personnel yellow-tape entrances and exits to the underground commutes. Underground, passengers are in a trance viewing grayed-out arrivals and departures on-screen itinerary data.

Confused, they grew flustered as well as impatient with transit officers who had no justifiable answers to their multiple proposed questions.

"Are the trains running? What's causing these delays?"

A yellow-hard-hat-wearing MTA Worker emerges. Pacing back and forth, he announces via a bullhorn:

"There is no train service at the moment. Please use alternate forms of transportation."

One confused woman toting two pieces of roller luggage tagged Amtrak, the one piece has a defective wheel so bad the roller luggage wobbles. She engages the MTA Worker.

"Is the Amtrak Train running?"

'Nothing is in service, Madam. The LIRR, New Jersey Transit, MTA, Path Trains, Amtrak – nothing. You may want to fly if you can get out of this Manhattan traffic." Says that courtesy–masked MTA Worker.

"What happened? I'm heading to my brother's funeral in Washington D.C. It's my last gift to him before he goes deep-six. He loved trains…" "Like I

THE N Y CONNIVERS SERIES

said. You may want to take the airplane. The trains are experiencing delays. Serious build-ups in the tunnels for more than an hour. Try Southwest Airlines, they go everywhere…Plus, two bags fly free!"

The woman departs, determined to use the elevator. She finds it difunctional – it opens but doesn't close. "It's jammed!"

She remarks, takes the street exit lugging her stuff, and forces her way past the NYPD barricades. Police with attack dogs and some with assault rifles pace deterring the woman. One dog pounces and sniffs her luggage as she departs.

Several levels deep, on platforms, as well as waiting areas, additional police dogs prowl. TV screens ramp up with the Breaking News: "The New York Subway is shut down and could last for several hours, possibly longer. Please use alternate forms of transportation."

That on-screen lower-thirds newscast rolls continually, upstaging the network's logo:

New Yorkers have never experienced these kinds of train service interruptions since Hurricane Sandy. Please use other means of transportation.

At the street level, vehicular traffic remains at a standstill. One hotdog vendor now racking up on

THE N Y CONNIVERS SERIES

sales and running out of ketchup, chili, sour craw, and mustard, blurts out:

"It's apparent the Subway is under siege. I hope this is not a terrorist operation or a repeat of 911."

A cop close by hearing the words "terrorist and 911" is nervously alerted. He readies his assault rifle while echoing over his shoulder radio:

"Someone just mentioned September 11th and terrorists, all in the same breath! Has anyone been informed of Counter Terrorism? The Bomb Squad?" Consequently, multiple cops become alerted, artillery combative, and radio happy.

THE N Y CONNIVERS SERIES

2

The gridlock builds expanding city-wide, towards the entire Eastside and now impeding the FDR Highway traffic flow. Not only multiple street blocks but multiple train stops in the NYC vicinity have now become an atrocious traffic nightmare. Compounded with cops and their bomb-sniffing dogs.

THE N Y CONNIVERS SERIES

To say the least, this whole thing is a total mess inundated with pedestrians, vehicles, tooting horns, and sirens.

At the Grand Central Terminal, the waiting areas have become elbow-roomed only with disgruntled unnerved potential passengers. Those giant display screens depicting train arrivals and departures all say canceled. More cursing and swearing erupts from those dissatisfied bombastic commuters. Some display one-finger signs to Train Service workers and the Amtrak Police.

For toddlers, it's not a happy traveling experience, as evidenced by several temper tantrum alarms. Their guardians and or parents pacify:

"Hush! Hush! Down by the station early in the morning. See the big puffer trains. They all say no, no! Today we don't go!"

Cooperative toddlers recite it fully after just a few tries.

The ones who don't get it show off their snooty noses. Police with their sniffing dogs roam and survey. Some law enforcement personnel investigate hawks on steroids. Counter-Terrorism Task Force lettering in milk-white, beams from their jackets. On the streets, surface transportation relaxes. From the air, the scene looks like the great Manhattan Standstill. MTA buses provide a shuttle service to avoid the traffic. Others blamed the Mayor for

THE N Y CONNIVERS SERIES

splitting up the streets in rural areas and installing bus lanes. Some complaining about that projected fare hike. Some even blamed the current US President.

On top of the private traffic reduction, these buses equipped with still cameras capture pictures of bus lane violators and the MTA later forwards a citation by mail.

A group of boisterous demonstrators emerge with signs and placards which read: *Stop the fare-hike. Give workers what's due to them!*

Complainants rant and rave: *The MTA should have kept those dinosaur buses instead of buying the state-of-the-art buses and then increasing the fare for ridership. We don't need their Wi-Fi. We have that at home. What we need is for them to stop taking advantage of us.*

THE N Y CONNIVERS SERIES

3

Underground, back at Broadway Avenue and the lower thirties, a handful of technicians in leftover computer booths huddle as they troubleshoot the underground connection problem. Which seemed to pierce a crater-sized hole in our operations. They are tasked with diagnosing what caused the glitch and trying to fix it swiftly.

THE N Y CONNIVERS SERIES

To them and other NYC authorities, whatever caused this has been and still is anonymous. Instead of the favorite mantra:
"Please stay away from the platform's edge."
It has now been replaced with:
"There is no train service at the moment. Please use shuttle buses upstairs or use alternate forms of transportation until service is restored."
Between Grand Central Terminal and 35th Streets at a subterranean level and inside a similar booth, multiple technicians fiddle with wires diagnosing what may have caused this service glitch.
Tension mounts as two Transit Police Officers claim responsibility for sabotaging the underground operations. At this time, though, their identity remains under wraps. The entire area outside Madison Square Garden is now littered with News Reporters, journalists, and all forms of TV, Radio, Newspaper editors, and mostly angry pedestrians.
"Whodunit" becomes the short prevailing question.
Never before in the history of New York City has the underground train service been so catastrophic. All elevators at Madison Square Garden are a no-go. So, are doors leading up and down stairwells.
"It's an inside job. That's what sources have been reporting. Even so, our network has not yet confirmed this."

THE N Y CONNIVERS SERIES

Says an eager and overwhelmed reporter at their station's news desk. People in Times Square watch this story unfold on those large-mounted TV screen monitors.

On the top floor at MSG, a uniformed NYPD Transit officer Clifton Reid drags a handcuffed elevator serviceman out of an elevator and unites him with three other handcuffed and muzzled hostages. This split-screen video feed also frames the mirrored top floor at Grand Central Terminal.

At this other location, Transit Officer Monica Tillerson replicates but on a higher level with three hostages in a corner, one woman and two men. Her gun can smell and it's Sulphur itches their nostrils. Still enamored with the limited information regarding these perpetrators. On the ground at MSG, The Police Commissioner is on edge, and so are multiple MTA officials.

"This is a siege-like non-other." Says a legal astute gentleman dressed in a suit and tie interviewee with a cable Channel. He draws a crowd while he writes meticulously on his clipboard.

THE N Y CONNIVERS SERIES

4

On the ground and across the way, the New York Mayor and his entourage arrive. News Reporters dart in his direction extending their microphones in his face.

"Mr. Mayor, how do you assess the situation and how soon do you think train service is going to be restored?"

THE N Y CONNIVERS SERIES

"We've never seen anything like this in the history of New York City. This has outclassed Hurricane Sandy." "I'm told. The trains are backed up in four Boroughs also affecting the schedules of the Staten Island
Ferry." Says
the reporter.
"Yes. Because there is no train service at Bowling Green Station and neighboring stations, the Staten Island Ferry remains docked in Staten Island. The Brooklyn and Queens tubes leading into Manhattan, I'm told are also clogged with stalled trains. This is not good for our city. However, we are told the train companies are working on it and we hope the service will be restored shortly." Says the Mayor.
"Some say it's an inside job?" Says the reporter.
"That has not yet been confirmed." Says the Mayor.
"We overheard the sabotage was carried out by two transit Police Officers." States the Reporter.
"Yes. That's what was reported. As I said before, this has not yet been confirmed." Says the Mayor.
"Mr. Mayor, thanks for talking with us."
Says the Reporter.
"You bet. As soon as we know more, we would be happy to provide an update."
The Mayor turns to leave.

THE N Y CONNIVERS SERIES

Another News Reporter presses with a microphone extended in the Mayor's face.

"Mr. Mayor, what would you say to the millions of commuters who are stuck in this transportation dilemma? Secondly, are there other accomplices besides those two Transit Police officers who've claimed responsibility?" Asks this News Reporter.

"Much of that reporting is still speculative as far as we are concerned. To your other question: We are restoring the service as soon as possible. You asked if there are additional accomplices. This condition is still under investigation. I would advise all train riders to find alternate means of transportation until this situation is resolved." Says the Mayor. "Thanks. Mr. Mayor." Says the Reporter. "You are welcome." Replies, the Mayor.

Outside MSG the perimeter is beleaguered with cops and additional bomb-sniffing dogs. The feed, on those ground floor monitors depicting the siege, grows dark and finally disintegrates. Techies on the ground scurry to reboot and or restore that lost transmission.

THE N Y CONNIVERS SERIES

5

Inside the NYPD office two Detectives: Jonathan Hobbs, nicknamed "Hans" who assumes everyone owes him a favor, and Jamie Johnson, nicknamed "J.J." a skilled street cop becomes informed during a phone call.

"Are they part of a domestic terrorist cell?

THE N Y CONNIVERS SERIES

Any Bombs?
Who's negotiating?"
"No one knows."
Replies an underling.
Who is behind this? Iran? Al Qaeda? Isis? Syria? China? North Korea? The Russians?"
Asks Hobbs.
"What do they want?
Did they say?
Two locations?
So, we are dealing with split-screen criminal sabotage on the NYC train systems?"
Jamie Johnson now with the receiver hanging in the air...
"It has been confirmed this is an Inside Job! Two Transit Police Officers. One from the Queens unit and the other from the Brooklyn unit." States Jamie Johnson.
"What do we have on those two?"
What's the phone number in that control room at MSG?... "
An underling still on the phone delivers...
"Got it!"
Says Hobbs as he writes the number down on a yellow pad. One of his underlings overhears and places the call. And the Grand Central Terminal. Hobbs scribbly writes it down and briskly passes it

to his partner Jamie Johnson. The phone facilitating that first call rings continuously. No one picks up. Hobbs is furious. "No answer?"
Asks Johnson.
"It seems the lights are on, but no one is at home. Wish that loser will pick up the darn phone."
Says Hobbs.
He continues.
"I'm going to be on location. Will you keep me posted?" "Locations!' Yells Johnson. "I've got MSG. You take GCT."
Says Hobbs.
"Wait! Since when we don't roll together? Is this the new normal? Splitting us up?"
Hobbs is still on the phone.
"It looks like we are going to have to call in hostage negotiators."
He says while staring at Johnson for some support.
"Great. Let's get to those twin sites before they do."
Says, Johnson.
They split up and head out briskly. Hobbs arrives at MSG via helicopter. NYPD officers surround this new arrival looking for answers. "Where is the negotiator?"
Asks Hobbs
"Stuck in traffic."
Says the Officer.

THE N Y CONNIVERS SERIES

"Where?" Asks Hobbs.

"Brooklyn Bridge. He is making it on foot."

Says an NYPD officer.

"Foot?"

Asks Hobbs, who, paces – peeved.

Meanwhile, multiple blocks away, Detective Jamie Johnson precedes the Negotiator's arrival at the Grand Central Terminal.

THE N Y CONNIVERS SERIES

6

With the perimeter of MSG littered with cops, the National Guard as well as multiple ranked cops with bomb-sniffing dogs, converge. A TV monitor from inside the ground floor lights up as if by accident transmitting static, and then LIVE footage. In conjunction, revealed inside the top

level at MSG several technicians seated and huddled in a corner handcuffed, except for a uniformed elevator operator. Clifton Reid keeps them at bay with a waving pistol.

Meanwhile, police officers are now trying to get to the top floor. However, their ascent is impeded; elevators don't work, and stairwell doors are still on lockdown. Hobbs tries desperately to make connections with the hostage-taker to no avail.

As the morning grows older, the lights in those two NYC hostage holdings locations are still on. Police officers are now trying desperately to get to that top-floor setting. Their access remains a non-starter from the ground up.

Police helicopters fly at low altitudes outside both buildings in a split-screen fashion and are seen on Times Square TV. Nothing much to see though as the morning's fog hinders clarity.

In the meantime, many riders are still stranded as they self-navigate their work commute. Several doctors working at hospitals in Manhattan are bused in and now housed at local hotels in Midtown.

Normally at this time of the morning: places of business in the city are fully operational. Plus, it's the first workday of the week. By this time, many New Yorkers were referring to it as Black Monday.

THE N Y CONNIVERS SERIES

Most businesses remain closed, partially open, and understaffed. Broadway Avenue and Seventh Avenue are convoluted with pedestrians and yellow cabs, now more than ever.

Fire engines on the run compete for most of the major street's real estate. Compounded with an abundance of law enforcement vehicles pursuing alternate routes. Even so, they are going nowhere fast, and like a vacuum, they suck up each other's idle fumes. The frustration on the faces of these NYC motorists looms. Sirens and the sound of vehicle horns crescendo. Underground, police surround the entrances and exits at 34th Street and Broadway.

THE N Y CONNIVERS SERIES

7

In the meanwhile, more information on those two Transit Police Officers drips. Right when optimism over their identity release soared. The monitors once transmitting the footage on the ground level at MSG went dark again.

Techies on the underground realized the computer chip that controls the switches at 34th Street revealed vacant slots. It was becoming apparent those two

THE N Y CONNIVERS SERIES

officers who recently claimed responsibility were more involved in the process than was reported and or believed.

"How the heck did they pull this off?"

Questioned one of those Techies who first discovered the missing computer slots. Throwing both of his hands in the air vividly displayed his frustration. Simultaneously, the missing computer information was also communicated to the Grand Central Terminal operators. They were appalled. The only people with access to those underground areas were those technicians, now held hostage. Information soon surfaced: they were abducted and lowered to the top floors of those separated and respective buildings.

At the time the transit police officers pulled this off at Penn Station underneath MSG. Clifton Reid was seen on a tear, disgruntled concerning the MTA. According to one eyewitness: He approached the technicians underground. At gunpoint, he demanded they immediately change the system passwords, reboot the system, and remove the computer chips. He instantly confiscated those chips.

He then made a phone call: "Monica!

Let the dogs out fully unleashed!"

Instruct Reid.

THE N Y CONNIVERS SERIES

It was later understood that his partner in the crime Monica Tillerson was located at Grand Central Terminal. She duplicated his efforts at her locale expeditiously.

Reid shuttled his hostages upstairs on an elevator handcuffed. On his way up the door opened and he was surprisingly joined by an Elevator Serviceman. Reid grabbed him at gunpoint. They arrived at the top floor.

"Kill the power on the elevator! Shut it down. Cease all stairwell traffic."

Said Reid to this Serviceman.

"Sir. The Knicks play the Nets here tomorrow night." Says the Serviceman.

"Do as I say. Shut them down! Let the Knicks play them at Barclays Center in Brooklyn." Says Reid.

IT WAS NOT ONLY ADDING UP at the NYPD Bureau but now it was more than law enforcement had bargained for in New York. There, they juggled phone calls after phone calls.

"Two NYC Transit Police officers completely shut the city down. This is real New York City Blues." Says a tourist wearing a Kansas City baseball cap while clutching his weekender roller luggage at Penn Station underneath MSG.

THE N Y CONNIVERS SERIES

People avoiding head-on got out of his way as he maintained his hustle and swagger going nowhere fast.

THE N Y CONNIVERS SERIES

8

Technicians kept on digging for answers. With the entire eastside still under gridlock, they sped up their operations to restore train service
at Grand Central Terminal to no avail. "Without that chip and those newly created passwords, we are stuck."

echoed one underground technician, who, at one point felt like he was the savior, destined to kickstart the underground connections.

Meanwhile, the hostage negotiator dispatched to GCT links up with the female Transit Police Officer by a private phone and attempts to broker a deal. After asking her what time she wanted, he felt she was demanding way too much. To make matters worse, he articulated her demands with a spokesperson wearing a Metro-North uniform. He, in turn, said her mandate was way over their heads. "Does she want us to pay everybody? That's ludicrous. If beggars were like horses, we all would ride." He says grandiloquently.

In the meantime, Monica Tillerson overheard his rhetoric through an unsecured line. Which was accidentally left open and on speaker mode. She felt they were overrated and too Trump-like. To counter she sarcastically said:

"No Deal!"

Thereafter, nothing that the negotiator said bore any fruit with the female hostage-taker. To say it mildly, everything arrived dead on arrival. It became evident they were not inclined to fulfill her wishes. Tillerson wanted it all or nothing.

THE N Y CONNIVERS SERIES

Back at Madison Square Garden, an NYPD officer approaches Jonathan Hobbs. "Are you the man in charge?"

"On the ground, I am."

Responds Hobbs.

"We've just received the word; the negotiator is still stuck on the Brooklyn Bridge."

Says the Officer.

"Anyone tried reaching the kidnapper?"

Asks Hobbs.

"Sir we tried. The elevators are out of service; lack of power and the exit doors at the stairwells are all locked. Plus, the outside of this building is too slippery to be scaled."

Responds to the Officer.

"Who's in charge of security?" Asks Hobbs.

"Michael Dean, Sir. He called in sick."

Says the Officer. "Who's next in command?" Asks Hobbs.

"He's stuck in traffic." "Who's under him?"

Asks Hobbs.

"We can't find him. He's missing."

Says the Officer.

"Who's the techie for Penn Station?"

Asks Hobbs.

THE N Y CONNIVERS SERIES

"I am!" Says an obese character. Hobbs instructs him.

"I need a line. A secure line. Lock all the other lines down."

Moments later, the Techie gives him the thumbs up. "Get the hostage-taker on the phone!" Commands Hobbs.

The Techie briskly hands the phone to Hobbs. Hobbs nervously looks into the phone at first. All eyes are now focused on him. Nervous at first, he finally gains his poise.

"Are you the Boss? Clifton Reid! My name is Jonathan, Jonathan Hobbs. You can call me Hans. I'm filling in for the negotiator. Not sure I could do as good a job. These guys are very sophisticated, but I'll try it. I'm not asking for much. But if both of us could come to a common understanding, both of us could come out of this with realized objectives. Firstly, is everyone okay? Does anyone need food or medical supplies, anything?

Hobbs waits for a response. There's none. "I wish you would talk back to me, Clifton Reid. This is a two-way street. I'll help you if you help me. You win, I win."

Hobbs continues.

THE N Y CONNIVERS SERIES

"Once again. This is Hans. Clifton, are you listening? If you can let those technicians you are holding go free, we might be able to kickstart this dilemma."

Still, there's no response from Clifton Reid. Inside that room, Reid sits back eating potato chips and drinking soda pop while the hostages wonder what their fate is going to be. They heard the negotiator's demands and saw a cold Clifton Reid refrain from responding.

THE N Y CONNIVERS SERIES

9

Meanwhile, an NYPD helicopter circles overhead.
"We've got a clean shot. We are ready to discharge."
Says the lead officer on board the aircraft.
"Heck no! Hold your fire!"

THE N Y CONNIVERS SERIES

Hobbs's response to the officer with an established laser focus. He shows some resilience in refraining but finally does so.

"But this nut decided not to even communicate with you. Why are you wasting your time?" Says the lead officer on that aircraft.

Hobbs tries once again to connect with Clifton Reid. "Mr. Reid. What are you asking for?" Asks Hobbs.

There's silence.

"I trust by your silence you are hearing me and clearly and collaborating with me." State Hobbs.

"Hans, I can see you now have aerial surveillance targeting me. Are you walking it back? I thought you were a man of your word. You've walked the beat in NYC bullying others. Don't play me! Do not only try to bully and even lie to me. If they make one mistake this whole deal goes awry. I will not hesitate to do what's in my power to grind this out." Says Reid.

Hobbs now senses scrutiny of his character flaws as a New York Cop deposited on center stage. Never before had Hobbs been attacked in a public setting since he signed up as an NYPD officer and endeavored to earn his stripes. Now to be stripped by an insider?

319

THE N Y CONNIVERS SERIES

"Please disregard, Clifton. That's just a law enforcement routine. What do you want?
If anything let us know, Clifton. Together we can solve this problem." Says Hobbs. "The promised pay increases." Says Reid.
"I can give you that myself. How much? Let's see if we can work this out. If that's what you want, we can call this whole thing off." States Hobbs.
"Hans. I can tell you are not any good at this. The pay increase for all MTA workers. Which we were promised six months ago. That pay hike! Period!" "I told you I wasn't good at this. Not sure I have that much in my Chase Bank Account. But I'm sure if you give me some time, I might be able to find some deep pockets. I'm sure the city is well equipped. Plus, you understand this is unrealistic for me to strike a magic wand. While I work on this for you, go ahead and send out technician John Mulroney. Give us something in good faith. There's a song I learned in Sunday school: So just give a little. Get a little…"
"Sorry Hans, I can't do that. I know that song… Mulroney is mine to keep. He is the database for the underground secrets… Amtrak, Metro-North, New Jersey Transit, Path Trains, LIRR. If it runs underground, he's got it. Even the rats! He's inside my back pocket until this deal is etched. Plus, I don't

trust you because I'm not feeling you. The MTA, Amtrak,
New Jersey Transit, The NYPD, even our guys, nobody. Nobody on the inside. Forgiveness is like a weapon. It's a strong one. So is justice."
The helicopter once circling above MSG has now aborted its mission and heads in the opposite direction. Hearing all this and sensing the stakes being raised.
Other officers look at Hobbs wondering:
What next? It seems like he has this! "You should have taken that bastard out!"
Says the MTA Spokesperson.
Hobbs isn't moved.
"Clifton, I can see we're working as a team now. That helicopter has just returned to base. Everyone listens to me from the ground up." Says Hobbs.
In the interim, A Transit Police Officer eavesdrops and buddies up with a stack of photographs depicting Clifton Reid.
Hobbs asks:
"You know Clifton Reid?"
"Yeah. Very well." Says the
Transit Officer. "Mixed motives?
Are you in on this?" Asks Hobbs.

THE N Y CONNIVERS SERIES

"Heck no! He lost his home. Foreclosure! That's when he went nuts! Over the edge! Ballistics!" Says, the Transit Officer.
"What kind of person is he? Has he ever been in the military? Iraq, Afghanistan, Syria, Grenada?" Asks Hobbs.
The Transit Police Officer responds:
"He's not your average warmonger."
"Are they ever average?"
"He's a darn fine officer. A family man. I can't believe he's doing this."
Hobbs returns the stack of photographs. The Transit Officer clutches them and in tears jerks a response:
"He's a leader. A good one. He's making the rest of us look bad. Terrible! We didn't sign up for this. It's like we all took an oath to defend New York City against anyone foreign or domestic."

THE N Y CONNIVERS SERIES

10

On the ground it simmers, as additional information on these two Transit Officers gone rogue pours in. A battle of words erupts volcanically between multiple train service executives mostly juggling for reliability.

THE N Y CONNIVERS SERIES

"Those two NYPD Transit officers, Clifton Reid, and Monica Tillerson... They have no authority over the New Jersey Transit, Amtrak, The LIRR, Metro-North, and the Path Trains. They police the subway trains, not us. They don't even own our computers or the tracks in our system. Yet, they circumvented and locked us down."
Says the agent for the New Jersey Transit.
"Why did they choose to compromise the underground confidential intel?"
Says a Path Train Representative. His organization suffers mostly from underground log jams as more than eighty percent of path trains are backed up in the tubes between New York and New Jersey.
"Disrupting the MTA is a felony punishable by up to 20 years. We are already losing millions per day since this entire sabotage began. It's not practical to issue a pay raise at this time. We've recently invested in over 500 brand-new Wi-Fi-ready buses citywide. Everybody knows that."
Says the MTA spokesperson while upstaging the Path Train Representative.
"Well, the siege continues..." Says an NYPD officer a few yards away. "Let me talk to Clifton Reid. He works for us. Reid owes us. He does."

THE N Y CONNIVERS SERIES

Says the MTA Spokesperson, approaching Hobbs and demanding the telephone device. Hobbs eyeballs him with a "this is not going to happen" signal.

The MTA Spokesperson is persistent. "I don't think that is going to work. It could further complicate things. Affecting this negotiating process." Says Hobbs.

"Ask him if we could meet him halfway. End the siege? Let the hostages go? Remove the siege and we'll make it good. First, beginning with the release of Mulroney. Then we can put the paperwork in cue for a review. That's a lot of money. You can't move a big ship with a drastic turn. You have to make a series of baby steps. This is New York City!"

Says the MTA Spokesperson.

Clifton Reid overhears through his unsecured line and responds.

"No deal. We'll keep it locked down until you deliver, Mr. Epstein. You were more interested in a fare hike. An operation that not only made you filthy rich but brings millions of dollars to this city. Why should we have to wait? Our mortgage doesn't. We have been waiting for... forever! When are you going to stand up and deliver? I'm working on it. That's what you said at our last meeting, remember?"

THE N Y CONNIVERS SERIES

Sensing leakage in their intel, NYPD personnel move quickly to disband. Hobbs wished he had nipped this tremor in the bud. Staying in control was his prerogative. Losing negotiation control to an insider could not only be his downfall but at this moment prove problematic. Letting control slip into the hands of the MTA an insider and subsequently slide to another the antagonist, Reid, could not only sabotage his already fragile negotiations. Fearing, Epstein could not only escalate his war on words but a face-off with his competition as combatant like the use of heavy weaponry.

"What do we have to do with you, Epstein? Just pay your bills so we all can go back to work." Says the Amtrak Spokesperson in his neatly pressed uniform, determined to turn up the heat.

"The MTA can barely acquire the funding they need for existing fast-track projects and avoid service cuts. Do you realize what you are offering that nut? What if he accepted our offer? That would certainly bankrupt the MTA.

Do you understand: Giving raises to approximately 75,000 employees plus back pay for six months would be like sealing off the underground for a long time if not indefinitely. He squares off at Hobbs and continues:

THE N Y CONNIVERS SERIES

"That deal you are about to make with Reid is just ludicrous and highly impossible."
That look on Hobbs' face says: *these agents need to chill so I can negotiate effectively with Reid, ending this standoff.* The Amtrak Spokesperson is resilient and interjects: "Yes. Even so, Epstein, you now move over 8.6 million passengers per day. Translating to over 2.65 billion rail and bus customers per year.
Don't you realize you are holding up our connections in Albany, Boston, Chicago, Washington DC, San Antonio, New Orleans, Los Angeles, San Francisco, Portland-Oregon, Seattle, and other major cities? Why don't you give the man what he wants and end this…?
So, we all can go back to work?" The MTA spokesperson, Epstein is rattled. Hobbs radio transmits.
"J.J. talk to me!"
Jamie Johnson is on the phone with Hobbs.
"Hobbs, this is not good. The negotiator pushed for Tillerson's surrender. As a result, she shot and killed those technicians, shot the negotiator and now she's at large. The building is littered with our own as the crime scene is under heavy investigation. As of now, we are not sure how many have been killed or if there are any survivors on that top floor. We are now in pursuit of Tillerson. Got to catch her…"

THE N Y CONNIVERS SERIES

Their phone connection goes fuzzy and eventually becomes filled with static. Hobbs hangs up and tries redialing. The phone connection does not cooperate.

THE N Y CONNIVERS SERIES

11

Jamie Johnson finally reconnects on that call with Hobbs.

"Hobbs, can you hear me?"

"This is better. Where is Tillerson now?" Replies Johnson and continues:

"We're now in pursuit of that bastard. There is no place she can hide. Those hostages at the top of the

THE N Y CONNIVERS SERIES

Grand Central Terminal were grotesquely shot and killed. Now, hauled out of there in body bags. She didn't have to do this! That negotiator she shot from that top floor was the nail in the coffin. He was collaborating with her on a deal. We're now backed up by a helicopter. However, none of us have GPS on her. Not as yet. The only clue is the left lane of the Brooklyn Expressway looks desolate. Motorists claimed they saw the runaway black SUV. Either she pushed those motorists out of the way or they accommodatively gave her the right of way."

Bang! Bang! The sound of two rounds comes in loudly through his alternate radio. Hobbs is rattled. "Johnson, hold on. It seemed all hell just broke loose on the top floor. I'll have to get back at you."

"What is going on? Were those motorists wrong? Did she show up at your location…?" Asks Johnson, not hanging onto Hobbs' last words. "I'll have to get back! Sounds like all hell just broke loose on that top floor."

Hobbs responds and is now occupied, investigating what just transpired at MSG.

ACCORDING TO NEW VIDEO.

Before Monica Tillerson abandoned her post on that upper level at GCT. She asked the lead technician

330

THE N Y CONNIVERS SERIES

for additional passwords to the underground connections. He pleads the fifth. Tillerson pulled out her gun, pointed it at him, released the trigger, and debated momentarily. He didn't budge.

"This is the last time I'm going to ask you to comply." She demanded.

Another technician, a woman, sensing what's about to go down, pleaded on her behalf – staying alive.

"Why are you trying to kill this innocent man? He has aided your cause by handing over the information you demanded. Hasn't he?" Said the Female Hostage. 'Shut up! Your turn is next." Said, Tillerson.

"How dare you refuse to give me what I asked?"

"What else do you want from me, blood?" Asked the female hostage.

Monica Tillerson pulled the trigger and shot the male technician in the chest.

Blood splattered all over that makeshift holding area. The other two technicians become recipients of his plasma. Tillerson then paced the room. She looked through the window and saw the landing littered with cops, artillery, and their vehicles. Peeved. She indicated to the female technician:

"You are next."

The standoff ensues as she returns some demeaning and threatening looks.

THE N Y CONNIVERS SERIES

"Do you share those changed passwords, which that fool decided to conceal?"

"That's not my department. Why didn't you get it from him before shooting him? That's amateurish… to shoot first and ask questions later. Don't you think?" She responds. "Do you have them?" Asked Tillerson.

"Yes. I do! So what? Are you going to shoot me if you don't get it?" She asks.

"No. I'll save you for dessert. I like Junior's cheesecake with strawberries layered on it." Tillerson then asks the other technician. He trembles like a leaf and points to the recently shot techie. The female techie whimpers feeling her time is coming soon. "Why don't you ask her?" He instructs.

She shakes her head "No" still trembling.

"What do you know then?"

Tillerson asked of her.

"Nothing. The desk where you met me is all I manage – HR."

"So, you know exactly who's holding up the promised pay increase?"

"I need that raise also. I think we all do. However, you don't have to put us through this torture and work stoppage."

THE N Y CONNIVERS SERIES

"That's not what I asked you. I requested information. Not a lecture on how things ought to be done under my watch."

"To answer your question: It could be multiple individuals. You can start with Epstein. You didn't get it from me. That man could have ties to the Mob. He acts like…"

"So, it's Epps. Sicilian tendencies? What about Amtrak?" She writes on a piece of paper and hands it over to Tillerson.

"You didn't get that from me."

Tillerson pops the other technician and shoots her too. Subsequently, Monica Tillerson's cell phone beeps. She checks the text message. It reads: "I'm outside in the back alley. Hurry!" "Now your long-awaited turn has come. It's time to kiss your world goodbye."

Says Tillerson as through the window, she pops the negotiator. Tillerson then opens the window on the opposite end and towards the alley. She lets herself down to the street level using a cord. There's a waiting SUV. She gets in.

THE N Y CONNIVERS SERIES

12

In the interim, the negotiator finally arrives at MSG via helicopter. Immediately after his deplaning. He squares off with Hobbs demanding his pre-assigned post. Oblivious to Hobbs, this negotiator Randolph Sinclair had been watching the late breaking news depicting the MSG operation during his helicopter ride to the crime

scene. Of course, Hobbs was not willing to give up that prestige. A status he cherished since before he joined the NYPD. "Who's in charge…? I'm now in charge." Demands Randolph Sinclair.

"Sorry, you are late. I've got this under control. Plus, I dislike insiders. It's due to an in-man that we are experiencing this NYC shutdown. How are you affiliated with Clifton Reid?"

Hobbs radios back to base.

"I want all the information on Monica Tillerson, let's throw out the net for a big catch.

Find out who she knows!

Who knows her?

Where does she spend time together?

Bars, nail salons, hair salons, restaurants, spas, gyms, strip clubs, clothiers, antique shops, churches, smoke shops, shooting ranges, racetracks, supermarkets, book clubs, and even the public library.

Her entire circle, kids, first and second cousins, everybody-Tillerson! We've got to get her.

When you get a lead. Hit me back." "No problem. I'm on it!"

Says Tillerson.

"I'm with you on this J.J." Replies Hobbs.

THE N Y CONNIVERS SERIES

Hobbs immediately refocuses his attention on the clear and present danger under and above his watch – the top floor at MSG.

As if by clicking an evil magic wand, that room at the top of MSG flips to gross darkness. Hobbs imagines the same scenario that was recently reported to him by Detective Johnson at Grand Central Terminal. Other cops and agents on the ground place Hobbs under a microscope; questioning his every move.

Some envy, some daring, and others seem not to care. Additionally, their body language says:

"What now? When does this end?" Randolph Sinclair departs from the scene after realizing he is not a fit inside the jigsaw puzzle.

Suddenly, several cops become animated. Including this NYPD officer, who, before Hobbs could issue additional orders, radios:

"Lights are off in that room at the summit. He could have killed them all. We should have let the real Negotiator clock in and do the job as he knows best. Are you certain that you have a handle on this, Hobbs? Because if you don't and this whole thing goes sour, we could all be dumped inside the trash can like curdled milk. I will not stand in this huddle and let that happen. My dad used to say 'Fish, cut

bait or get out of the way!' I know how to execute the art of the deal." Says the NYPD Officer.

"Go ahead! Call in Ghostbusters…"

Replies Hobbs.

"I can. You don't know who I know in the bureau as well as internal affairs."

That statement doesn't sit well with Hobbs; still finding his way. Challenged, Hobbs gets on his radio and connects with the hostage-taker, Clifton Reid.

"Clifton Reid?"

Hobbs continues:

"This is Hans. Does anyone need medical assistance, food, or water? "

"No need to worry about us, Hans. I've got this! However, you are running out of time. Do you wear a watch? If not, every smartphone is equipped with a time-telling App."

"If there is an alternate deal to be made, let's make it now."

Says Hobbs.

"The Deal? No substitute. The deal, Hans!"

Hobbs is unnerved by that response. That cantankerous NYPD officer is stapled, catching every word in this two-way pow-wow.

"If you need time to produce a compromise that's okay. However, in the meantime, I could have

someone bring you some food, snacks, and meds. He looks over at the NYPD officer.

"Or I could deliver those to you personally." Hobbs continued.

"Hans, or should I call you Hobbs instead? You made a deal, man! No need for tinkering with it. We don't have all day. Your word is dripping like water from a basket." Reminds Reid.

Now, that same NYPD officer is joined by other cops and agents on the ground with eavesdropping eyes locked in on Hobbs as if they didn't hear what he just declared.

"You are not only putting yourself in harm's way but for us as well. What if when you go up there, he comes down to us unhinged? That man is armed and dangerous. He orchestrated a lockdown in New York City. Why are you appeasing this psychopath? Look at the mess he has thrown around our city." Says that NYPD officer.

The legal astute notetaker, still personalizing his clipboard now logs the scene in shorthand.

Meanwhile, those challengers are on the ground holding their breath waiting for a response from Reid which may turn the tide. His second radio on the next hand transmits and then suddenly disrupts. "Clifton, the clock is running."

THE N Y CONNIVERS SERIES

"You don't scare me, Hans. I'm no longer a slave to fear…!"

THE N Y CONNIVERS SERIES

13

During this extended and brewing standoff between the NYPD and hostage-taker Clifton Reid as well as their pursuit of his accomplice Monica Tillerson. The tragedy spun like a sleeping tap in the public milieu. Some claimed:

THE N Y CONNIVERS SERIES

The Mayor assumed the underground connections could be interrupted for days on end. In so doing multiple shuttle buses were immediately put into play, bringing passengers from Queens across the bridges into Manhattan and doing a roundabout. The same happened for commuters from Brooklyn as well as from New Jersey.

From Staten Island, the Staten Island Ferry was canned, and those commuters were brought across the Verrazano Bridge into Brooklyn and then shuttled across the Brooklyn and Manhattan Bridges into Manhattan via buses.

Assistant professor Marcus Billings of urban planning at New York University and a Transit expert cautioned against pinning down a time limit for the resumption of NYC train service.

"It's a gamble to put a duration on it."

He said.

"Getting train service up and running again is going to take some time. Even if the hostage-takers surrender. There has to be a cooling-off period before trust is reestablished by commuters and workers alike." He continued.

Even though some disagreed with him, this was his lane, and he wasn't going to be derailed by anyone, not even the Mayor of the largest city on the planet. Experts from the Metro in Washington and Chicago

THE N Y CONNIVERS SERIES

and even Marta in Atlanta produced suggestions about the period to get the system back up and running. Yet, Billings felt they were way off; not understanding the complexity of the New York underground. A system, proven to be out of tune with the constant grinding of wheels for years. It was a given, that when this system on which the MTA Subway was built and operated for decades was not built to withstand escalated demands of ridership and speed. Resulting in constant weekend patchwork to its fabric. Thus, causing excessive re-routings and inconvenience to riders.

According to Mr. Billings:

"When this MTA Subway system was constructed. No one ever thought there would be a need for fast track, Wi-Fi ability, schedule listings, and even dominated bus lanes on most city streets.

Compounding it all, ridership has increased tremendously not only by New Yorkers but by tourists as well. Contributing to the wear and tear of the system. That's one reason why this weekend's maintenance of the system has proven to be problematic. The upkeep demands are staggering. They are always fixing something. Mainly on weekends.

Most riders end up being shuttled on buses which takes a much longer time limit to get riders from

THE N Y CONNIVERS SERIES

point "A" to point "B" at a time when they would rather relish a relaxing commute." On the other hand, some MTA insiders felt these stats were an overreach for Mr. Billings.

THE N Y CONNIVERS SERIES

14

The standoff between hostage taker Clifton Reid and law enforcement maintained a clear and present danger. While his accomplice Monica Tillerson remained at large. Tillerson for over 24 hours like a vacuum has now sucked the air out of the
situation and led Law Enforcement on a wild goose chase.

THE N Y CONNIVERS SERIES

Until now, not too many knew of Monica Tillerson's identity. The news broke regarding her profile in the media overnight not only in the New York Times but on multiple TV channels: Monica Tillerson aka MT grew up in Astoria, Queens. Her dad Ralston Tillerson was a train station clerk with the MTA for more than 30 years. Her mother Candice Haynes-Tillerson, a train engineer for the same tenure met Ralston on the job and tied the knot months later.

Candice worked on just about every train line the MTA facilitated. Her rut was often discussed around the dinner table as she was familiar with every inch of rail those iron train cars encountered.

The passage through the tubes from Brooklyn and Queens and into Manhattan was always of interest to young Monica. She propped up and grinned every time trains became a topic of conversation at the dinner table. For some time, it baffled her how the MTA was able to construct tunnels underground and protect them from water leakage.

The effects of Hurricane Sandy on its infrastructure in 2012 validated her fear as water surged inland and caused a total shutdown of the system. It was then on Sunday 28, 2012 that the MTA announced at a press conference that all subway, LIRR, and Metro-North services were suspended at 7 PM, and

THE N Y CONNIVERS SERIES

bus service two hours later in anticipation of the storm.

Some closures last for an extended duration. To Monica, it was an MTA wake-up call. Claiming they had been lax when it came down to designing the underground's infrastructure.

On the other hand, she saw the scenario of trains racing through those underground tubes as giving her the perspective of a spirited individual navigating a challenging life.

Monica Tillerson was never married. Recently, when her name made news as one of the hostage-takers in the subway siege, her son Rick Tillerson had just left for college to become an engineer.

He too, like the two generations that preceded him had an affinity with trains and envisioned after college landing an elite position with the MTA. In his grandmother's will, he inherited her journalized parchment documenting her daily underground trips. Monica Tillerson, additionally, was a passionate advocate for the Springfield, Massecuites Women's Movement.

THE N Y CONNIVERS SERIES

15

Monica Tillerson saw herself as a born leader. One who created an individual blueprint to get her way in and out of difficult situations. A fan of David Schwartz's writings – *The Magic of Thinking Big*. At an early age, she mastered the art of negotiating. After being a train conductor for five years, she persuaded her boss to become a cop assigned to the MTA. He liked

THE N Y CONNIVERS SERIES

her in that engineering role. Taken aback by her journalizing capabilities.

She was quick with a pen and paper. In defending her decision to become a Transit Police Officer, according to a source close to her: As the only child, she was not only spoiled rotten by her parents and neighbors but acquired smarts far superior to those kids at her school as well as in her neighborhood.

As a ten-year-old, Monica visited abandoned train tracks, wrecks, and stationery-customized train cars, taking notes. Visualizing one day she would drive a runaway train. One which could travel at least 320 MPH. Bringing her vision closer to reality, Monica took a trip to Paris, France. After exploring Paris, she boarded a bullet train to Niche, Cannes, and Grasse in Southern France. Returning to the US, Monica cherished the velocity at which those trains in Europe rolled. It was then she enlisted as an NYC train engineer. Holding down that position for about half a decade.

"I've seen way too many passengers get away with too much. Everything from fare evasion to vandalism and panhandling."

The source also claimed: that Tillerson, if she had been in that employ during the tenure when trains and subways were graffitied, those text-free pundits

would have faced the consequences. She viewed their actions back
then as a total disregard for the property of someone else's.
Tillerson and her partner in crime Clifton Reid worked the subway beat together for years. They were seen frequenting the 1, 2, and 3 trains as well as the 4, 5 and 6. At base camp, they were both known as the constant note-takers.
Tillerson, at the time when she sabotaged the underground connections along with Reid. It was said she missed multiple payments on her cherished black Chevy Tahoe SUV.
During those hard times, she resorted to hiding her SUV in neighbor's garages, to avoid having it repossessed.

THE N Y CONNIVERS SERIES

16

Clifton Reid, on the other hand, migrated from Jamaica to New York during the era when Afro hairstyles, bell-bottom pants, and platform shoes dominated. Reid came from a family of two pastors. In school, he was referred to as PK 2.

THE N Y CONNIVERS SERIES

While at Manchester High, Clifton excelled in soccer as well as cricket. Additionally, he was always the go-to guy when it came down to working out complex problems.

Immigrating to the US he soon thereafter became naturalized. It was then he joined the MTA. Reid began his employment with the MTA as a train conductor and eventually worked his way up to Transit Police. He saw himself not bullying but working aggressively to reach his quotas. He cited viciously, thus enhancing his skill, and accelerating swiftly up the chain of leadership in his vocation.

His part-time scholastics included aeronautics at Vaughn College outside La Guardia Airport. He married Theresa Morgan, who paved the way for his US naturalization. Although born in the Caribbean Island, Jamaica. Reid saw himself as a "Yankee" and fathered two sons and a daughter. His daughter Megan, the apple of his eye and split image of her dad was privileged as the rose between two thorns. She not only knew it but lived it.

Theresa, a registered nurse and a great one, worked extended hours mostly during the graveyard shift at a local Manhattan hospital. Clifton Reid had always spoken extensively as an advocate for human rights. At the time when Reid embarked on sabotaging the train connection, he had missed multiple payments

THE N Y CONNIVERS SERIES

on his Brooklyn brownstone home and saw it plummet into foreclosure.

Additionally, there was much talk about a pending fare hike by the MTA. This didn't sit well with most of their ridership, including Reid.

On the other hand, the long-awaited pay increase promised by the MTA wagged the dog. Caught up in all this denial, the Reids found themselves pressured to fund their daughter Megan's initial tuition at Columbia Law School.

THE N Y CONNIVERS SERIES

17

It wasn't long before FBI agents raided the home of Clifton Reid in Brooklyn. They readily confiscated computers, external hard drives, written journals, thumb drives, audio, and video recordings, cameras as well as other gadgets.

THE N Y CONNIVERS SERIES

At the time of the raid on that early morning at dawn.

They also took into custody Theresa Reid and their three young adult kids. They claimed these arrests were conducted on suspicion of collaborative criminal sabotage of the underground connections.

Theresa Reid claimed: that neither she nor her kids knew anything about or had anything to do with the hostage situation still underway at Madison Square Garden, an extension of this train line's sabotage. The FBI did not buy into their non-affiliation with the disclosures of the crime. To support their arrests, they told the Reids: that this hostage situation had to be a well-thought-out process. Possibly lasting more than a full year.

Furthermore, they had no qualms about letting Theresa know if her husband was going to pull off such an ordeal of this magnitude. It was almost impossible for a wife who lived in the same house and possibly slept together in the same bed, not to have seen or heard anything leading up to such a horrendous criminal activity.

The young adult kids also claimed they did not know what these going on which led to the sabotage of the train systems.

The FBI didn't buy their story either. To cover their butts, the Bureau placed that entire family under

arrest pending their confession or willingness to cough up pertinent information.

During that raid in Brooklyn. Additional FBI agents raided the home of Monica Tillerson in Astoria, Queens. They entered the home in takedown style. Fearing her, Monica, who was still at large might still be residing there and armed.

Unfortunately, and fortunately for them, she wasn't home at the time. However, her son, Rick was. He had a newbie at college. Rick claimed: that he knew nothing about his mother's plan to disrupt the train service. Rick informed them that his mother was a good woman, loved her church, and was a law-abiding citizen. The FBI envisioned a completely different story. The fact that she killed three hostages and the negotiator at the GCT kidnapping, and fled was the complete opposite of who he thought his mother was. When asked if he knew of her whereabouts. He said:

"No."

Still, they saw him as an accomplice. They eyed, searched, and later towed the black SUV. Inside they discovered blood droplets on the seat linked to one of the hostage's DNA.

Furthermore, Rick's computer's background displayed a photo of the # 7 train which ran from Flushing to Manhattan. Additionally, his Facebook

THE N Y CONNIVERS SERIES

page was inundated with pictures of antique as well as new trains. "This kid has way too much affiliation…" Said one of the FBI agents to another. With Rick already in handcuffs, they confiscated computers, cameras, external hard drives, journals, and thumb drives, along with an appointment book detailing Monica's upcoming visits with her neurologist.

THE N Y CONNIVERS SERIES

18

Outside MSG, NYPD helicopters circle its summit. On the ground, onlookers: some run for cover, some maintain their distance. While others got immersed in the thick of things. Some of the latter display their advocacy towards Clifton Reid. They came out of the closet after the news broke that Reid was angry with the MTA and documented a laundry list. Headlined:

THE N Y CONNIVERS SERIES

The projected fare hike upstaging a promised raise to its almost 100,000 workers.

Hobbs on the ground, and oblivious to the reasons for Reid's' emerging support, remains in negotiating mode. Yet, after being torn to shreds by Reid's assassination of the detective's character.

"Clifton, are you hearing me?" Asks Hobbs.

"I am. Hans? I thought you fell asleep at the wheel!" Responds Clifton Reid, who continues:

"What's going on? I thought we had an agreement. I thought you were going to hold off these flying predators at bay."

"Clifton Reid, like I told you. There's a time constraint. You've not turned over John Mulroney to us. So, it's now out of my hands. Totally out of my control."

"So, you are going to take out these hostages? I mean have your Ariel squad shoot them. I could make that very easy for you."

"I'm not saying that's how I want this to go down." Says Hobbs.

"So, what are you proposing, Hans? Speak now or forever hold your peace!" Asks Reid.

"What are your grievances, Clifton Reid? Your real grievances?"

Asked Hobbs.

About this time, Reid went mute on Hobbs.

THE N Y CONNIVERS SERIES

It was also oblivious to Hobbs that Reid had watched the Cable News on iPhone regarding the FBI-conducted raids. Now with a few power bars left he elected to conserve the energy. Reid saw during that raid, his items confiscated, along with his three kids arrested and hauled away by the Feds. He remained not a happy camper after watching this occurrence. Anyway, he was able to compartmentalize those raids until now.

With those helicopters still surveilling Reid walked across to that secured phone and dialed Hobbs. "Hans. You have asked what my grievances were. I thought you would have known by now. However, if you have not already been informed. For your benefit as well as your cronies, let me reiterate. I'll release to you my MTA laundry list as an addendum." Clifton Reid methodically went through his MTA laundry list. Itemized as if they were prefaced as bulleted points. To him and Monica Tillerson, these were already their documented talking points as written in their confiscated journals.

THE N Y CONNIVERS SERIES

19

Multiple MTA officials on the ground at MSG were privy to that heated exchange between Hobbs and Reid. They were aware that the MTA which controlled the New York Subway system, LIRR, Metro-North, Bridges, and Lanes on multiple NYC major streets could have done a better-blanketed job. That potential fare hike

360

although now a point with riders didn't sit well and cast extended blame on the city.

Even so, they had at the moment a more important task at hand: The mission of restoring the underground connections. This weighed heavily on their minds. Yet, they were not prepared to fulfill promises to their workers. Not at this moment, they were focused on reeling it in rather than doling it out. Tillerson and Reid's demands were DOA.

During a subsequent phone call from Reid to Hobbs. Reid questioned how Hobbs wanted him to deliver John Mulroney.

In the meantime, Reid asked Mulroney to write down all the recreated passwords for those underground connection systems.

"Concerning Mulroney?"

Reid asked Hobbs, with the helicopters still hovering.

Hobbs deliberated silently.

Reid continued:

"Do you want him delivered dead or alive?"

"Clifton, this man has a family. Young kids. They would be happy to see him alive again." Says Hobbs.

"I have a family too, Hobbs. If you want Mulroney, you are going to have to release my wife and three

THE N Y CONNIVERS SERIES

kids. Set them free. An eye for an eye. A tooth for a tooth."

States Reid.

"Not sure I can make that happen. As you know a move like that is completely out of my control and in the hands of the SDNY and the FBI." "Hans, you have access to a phone, don't you? Use it! I take it that you have multiple ways of communicating my demands. And while you are at it, add the release of Rick Tillerson to your list. He's part of the deal."

Hobbs, baffled as to Reid's knowledge of external affairs while he's secluded on this top floor, looks for answers.

The Police Commissioner, now nearby and overhearing the conversation, gives a "Yes" nod to Hobbs urging him on.

In the meanwhile, Reid notifies Hobbs through that line of communication:

"Hans, you have only 60 minutes to make this happen."

Hobbs looks at his watch and responds: "Clifton, this is not accomplished by the waving of a magic wand. We are going to need at least 2 hours." "You have a full hour. The city wants to see this ordeal ended sooner rather than later. Doesn't it?" Demands Reid.

The police commissioner once again gives Hobbs a "Yes" nod.

THE N Y CONNIVERS SERIES

Hobbs quickly responds:
"Hang in there. I'm working on it! Understand this is a weekend and all city offices are closed."

THE N Y CONNIVERS SERIES

20

Inside that summit room at MSG, Reid turns the heat up on his hostages. After those two shots rang out earlier Hobbs reintroduced the helicopters to see if those cops on board could get a peep inside that room with the aid of their aircraft's floodlights. Tactfully, Reid had that view sealed off with the cubicles. Nothing to see, the cops backed off.

THE N Y CONNIVERS SERIES

Moments later after the helicopters retreated, Reid opened the tiny window and tossed out John Mulroney's blood-soaked jacket. Previously, when Reid shot Mulroney in the leg, he used the technician's jacket as a bandage for his leg wound and soaked up the blood that splattered on himself. That jacket fell on the ground level in that huddle careened with Hobbs, the Commissioner, and spokespeople for those service-affected train lines.

Since those two shots rang out on that top floor, Hobbs has been desperately trying to contact Clifton Reid, until that previous conversation with Hobbs went mute. He avoided those negotiating calls. Reid, at that time, felt like he had the upper hand. That floor kept ringing intermittently. When the jacket landed on the ground. Hobbs took a fact-finding look at it. Not only was it saturated with blood but bore the embroidered lettering – John Mulroney on its breast pocket.

That NYPD officer, looking over Hobbs' back asked: "So, he sent you blood-soaked clothing?"

Amtrak spokesperson intercepts. "No. He sent us a blood cloth."

"Reid. That rat. He turned on his department and then put them in a vice."

Said the Police Commissioner.

THE N Y CONNIVERS SERIES

The helicopters returned for yet another peep into that top floor.

"Reid, this is Hans. We received your little blood-soaked gift. Is everyone safe? Is Mulroney alive? We can send our Medics in to perform needed first aid." Meanwhile, cops from one of the helicopters deplane onto the roof looking for access into the building.

"Do you need bandages? Food? Water? Anything?"

"Hans, all of this could have been avoided. You and your guys decided to hang me out to dry. I don't like your games. Don't play me. You have proven you cannot keep your word. Water in a basket." *Bang!*

Reid shoots Mulroney in the other leg. The helicopters increase their altitude. Hobbs on the ground hears the gunshot echo.

"Hans, we need a pair of crutches. If you need Mulroney now, you can have him delivered as-is. If you delay meeting my demands you may need a shovel and body bag. Have it your way." The cops gain limited access through the roof now able to overhear Reid's movements. However, the door, seen on the building's blueprint leads to the floor where Reid is sealed off.

THE N Y CONNIVERS SERIES

21

In the meanwhile, as Reid continued terrorizing his hostages. The NYPD snipers were constantly working on gaining access through the roof at MSG. Meanwhile, Monica Tillerson was on the run. According to New York's Mayor, when it comes to Tillerson:

"We are fighting an enemy and we don't even know where she is. We need to catch her now!"

THE N Y CONNIVERS SERIES

In the interim, the FBI released Reid's family from custody. Theresa Reid, her daughter, and two sons were now poised to sleep in their beds. However, Rick Tillerson the son of Monica Tillerson was still under arrest. No doubt, law enforcement wanted to make sure Monica Tillerson was in custody, either dead or alive before releasing Rick.

The late-breaking news about Reid's family release saturated the airwaves. Inside that hostage room, Clifton Reid used whatever was left of his iPhone's power bar to tune in. He watched the news in a speaker mode away from his huddle.

Above him and still concealed, cops worked tirelessly cutting through that roof. While Reid tuned in to the news, argued with the hostages, and communicated with Hans on the ground. Those cops above were eventually able to tap into that room's atmosphere using small tubes. They were now privy to his next moves as well as Hobbs on the ground. Hobbs, on the other hand, felt by helping get Reid's family out of police custody Reid would be more willing to comply with demands. Even so, that favor did not move the needle toward letting even the injured John Mulroney go. Associates of Hobbs blamed him. Accusing him of letting himself get conned by Clifton Reid. Some of them even stuck

THE N Y CONNIVERS SERIES

it to him that they would not have initiated any dialog to have Reid's family released. They felt he should have used their release as bait, hook, and sinker.

As far as Reid was concerned, the release did not include his partner-in-crime son, Rick Tillerson. Therefore, in his eyes, Hobbs had not done enough. Not fulfilling that segment of the deal.

"A broken link still existed in the chain of demands." Said Reid, who entertained the epiphany, that the MTA had not dealt with his blanketed demands – dealing with the proposed wage hike. Therefore, purposing in his heart, he was going to dig in, sticking to his guns. Hobbs and Reid engaged in a nefarious debate over the rules of the game.

THE N Y CONNIVERS SERIES

22

As detective Jamie Johnson and other NYPD officers searched by land, sea, and air looking for Monica Tillerson, through connecting streets in Brooklyn and elsewhere. An Amtrak train, parked at Penn Station rolled out of that establishment.

By the time authorities were alerted it was gaining steam northbound. According to sources, this was

THE N Y CONNIVERS SERIES

the last train to pull into that station, after the underground connections went awry. It was believed at the time it departed Penn Station it was unmanned. One of its doors was partially opened and a manifest is yet to be released and verified.

It was also factored into the rollout that the brakes on that train were disabled mechanically. While the speculations surrounding this train's departure surfaced. The runaway train was speedily heading northbound towards upward of the Hudson River.

It was soon determined from the air that the engineer at the helm was Monica Tillerson, still clothed in that blood-stained Transit Police Officer's uniform. Multiple helicopters now joined in the aerial pursuit. On the ground, police cruisers joined in with the first train stop at Croton Harmon Station. For the train, this stop became a bypass. The runaway train bolted through there at rapid speed. In the interim, Coast Guard Cutters and other combated ships blanketed the Hudson River but in futility.

While police cruisers armed with SWAT teams lined the streets adjacent to tracks parallel to the Hudson River.

Helicopters soared up above in pursuit of that Amtrak train. Ground transportation with law

THE N Y CONNIVERS SERIES

enforcement decals rushed outside along the tracks. In total, they couldn't stop it.

THE N Y CONNIVERS SERIES

23

With the platform at Croton Harmon in the rearview of the train now running away at 75 MPH in 50 MPH zones with sparks flying off those rails. Amtrak authorities feared a collision with a southbound freight train sharing a fork lane and bearing down miles away

and reportedly transporting hazardous chemicals. If they arrived there at the same time that collision could be catastrophic.

This cargo train was also toting automobiles and coming full steam ahead. More so it was speculated, according to authorities, that the Amtrak train either had no brakes or that its brake system was tampered with as an excessive amount of brake fluid was discovered where the train was parked at Penn Station.
"We are still hopeful that its brake functions. If it doesn't, we are up the creek!" Said an Amtrak official.
"We need to stop this train. On this route, we share tracks with the Pacific Coast. We rent from them. They have priority over these tracks."
It became evident according to that train's manifest and later verified by a circling helicopter, that there were three couples on that train. Jamie Johnson, onboard that aircraft spotted them inside the dining car. About this time, the train passed through a shrubbery-thick neighborhood. The helicopter rerouted.
Later, they were back. After checking with Amtrak, it was confirmed the three couples onboard all used sleeping cars.

THE N Y CONNIVERS SERIES

Additionally, they could have gotten stuck onboard in the aftermath of the NYC train service dilemma. Their destination was Newark, New Jersey. Which, was
supposed to be the next stop on that train bound for Washington, DC after that NYC layover. The train was headed northbound instead. Now gunning towards Poughkeepsie Station, the next stop on its normal route and about 3 miles away.
The platform was getting crowded. Now yellow taped-off, onlookers remained persistent. On the southbound tracks, a parked Metro-North train resided. Station officials feared this runaway train, if not able to switch tracks before entering this station could collide with it head-on.
Luckily, it didn't speed through that station way above its speed limit, leaving sparks in its path. Some of those onlookers applauded. Some held their breath with their hands covering their mouths.
Even so, law enforcement personnel and Amtrak officials gathered, and all agreed that was a tedious encounter to witness. As they signaled for Monica Tillerson to stop and or slow down. Tillerson, on the other hand, defied their orders. Her hustle was way too much for their halt as that train was gone screeching towards its next station stop, Rhinecliff.

THE N Y CONNIVERS SERIES

24

The Amtrak interoffice engineer continued with his antics. Pressuring law enforcement to deliver on his behalf.
"What if this train blows up in a residential neighborhood?"
He questioned.
"Is there a bomb, onboard? Who else is on it?"
Asked an upstate New York Sheriff as he raced

THE N Y CONNIVERS SERIES

towards the Poughkeepsie Station followed by a convoy of Sheriff cars.

"Gosh. They look sick to me. If they were to be thrown into a rescue net. They possibly lack the strength needed to catch it."

He continued while talking over his radio.

"We need to find a way to derail it before it gets to Albany."

Reports an office engineer at the Albany Station. "Albany is like our hub. We can switch the tracks here when it comes through. I know there have been talks about catching her alive but at this point, we need to do what's best for Amtrak. Not for this criminal." He continued.

"Before entering the station there is a steep incline. Why not derail it during that ascent? That way its speed would be minimized."

Said another in-office engineer at the Albany station, pacing in his booth.

"How about crossings?"

He asked an engineer at Penn Station.

"I can't see how we got sucked into this MTA dilemma. This should not have been our war." He continued.

"We've closed off all the crossings. That's no place to derail a train. Lawsuits will push us out of business."

THE N Y CONNIVERS SERIES

That engineer at the Albany station, responds. "First we need to find a way of getting those three couples from the train."
Says the Penn Station engineer.
"Why didn't you guys take them off the train at Penn Station? Why was that door still open? Who cleaned up?"
Asks the engineer at Albany Station. "I don't clean the trains. I just direct them where to go." He responds.
"So, why don't you direct this one where to go?"
He responds.
The train continues to speed away. Now at three times the speed limit. Civilians crowd the crossings. Some just to see this runaway train engineer - Monica Tillerson. Some to watch a LIVE movie for free. Some to say:
"I was there!"
Some, mainly to be seen in the barrage of Television coverage. Some even brought their kids to see this runaway mega train.

THE N Y CONNIVERS SERIES

25

Amtrak personnel were ardently thinking ahead. They had not yet gotten out of this NYC debacle and now this. It was severely affecting the company's bottom line.

After Poughkeepsie, they concentrated heavily on bringing this to a halt at Albany if it cleared Rhinecliff.

THE N Y CONNIVERS SERIES

This stop was their normal change of crew station, a reconnection for trains heading to either Boston or Chicago. A stop where the Lakeshore Limited train line normally would split into two halves to now accommodate those separate destination routes. Additionally, this stop facilitated multiple run-off tracks. To facilitate the mechanical service of the trains. To complicate the process. Amtrak authorities were now puzzled. They were not aware if: Monica Tillerson would choose to embark on the Boston route or the Chicago route. If for any reason they were unable to stop this train at Albany.

Even so, law enforcement in conjunction with Amtrak further expanded their game plan.

Information surfaced, Monica Tillerson, was at one point very well connected in Springfield, Massecuites. Envisioning that could be her resolute homecoming, and regrouping with members of her women's movement might complicate catching her. Therefore, the train authorities fortified the Albany to Springfield route. While additional cops camped out in Springfield in anticipation.

That Poughkeepsie stop was now in hindsight. Albany weighed heavily on the minds of authorities even though Rhinecliff was next.

THE N Y CONNIVERS SERIES

However, still onboard were these three couples. Getting them off this train already proved problematic for those air lifters.

An Albany derailment could be devastating for Amtrak if they in the process took the lives of these senior citizens. Yet, they were determined to stop this train at Albany.

THE N Y CONNIVERS SERIES

26

It wasn't long before a helicopter manned by NYPD began lowering a net to rescue the three couples from the train. Coming close, those rescuers focused on the dining car, where those three couples huddled. Rescuers instructed the couples via an amplified audio system to move toward and between cars. There the net would drop

THE N Y CONNIVERS SERIES

and all they needed to do was to grab on tightly to the net, and they would be rescued.

The couples are excited to detrain. Yet, they expressed their reluctance to take that leap of faith. Unsure if any of the couples suffered from a heart condition. Their rescuers did not alert them: the train would no more be after Albany as was planned. They were further instructed to leave their carry-on luggage behind. "Take nothing with you!" Was the instruction?

Of course, that didn't sit too well with those elderly women who were still holding on to their pocketbooks and cemented in their ways. One of those women refusing to heed the warning went back and retrieved her carry-on. The net dropped and after multiple tries, the first couple between train cars was airlifted. The one with her carry-on absorbed most of the time while the train was railing in the open terrain. Soon it encountered a massive stretch of tall shrubbery. Attempts were futile as the train also picked up speed towards Albany Station. During this interlude, the two couples argued over who should have gone first in line to be rescued.

Continued rescue attempts by helicopter were curtailed. The train entered the station full speed ahead just like it had done at prior stations in the route.

THE N Y CONNIVERS SERIES

27

Back at MSG, three NYPD snipers creatively descended and landed on that top floor. They swiftly traveled the distance with guns outstretched towards Clifton Reid's assumed direction.

Tension mounts on their part. On the ground, Hobbs, imaginatively by phone kept Reid busily engaged. Hobbs articulated what was like music to

THE N Y CONNIVERS SERIES

Reid's ear: Reid's ultimate demands. Hobbs assured Reid that he would get him whatever he wanted at this point. Reassuring these demands would soon be met and vice versa the MTA. Even though Hobbs had already lost some credibility with Reid. This Transit Police Officer endowed and stellar in leadership still believed and was eager for Hobbs to keep pushing that big-thick envelope at the MTA.

Hobbs had walked it back on multiple occasions during this negotiation process. Now it seemed he had sanitized his hands.

Even so, his herky-jerky tactics still irritated Reid who at this point was looking for tranquility in negotiations. Anyway, Hobbs through his brilliance and cunning had Reid's listening ear.

Right when Reid was buying, another helicopter circled the building's perimeter. Tossed to an FRO, Reid felt he had inherited not only an earful but an empty-handed Hobbs. So, he punted. First, he took out the other hostages with multiple shots except for the Elevator Serviceman who was missing in action. Moments prior, Reid heard a sound in the direction of the elevator and sent the elevator serviceman to investigate.

Now peripherally and through his sixth sense, he overheard multiple and varied footsteps coming in

his direction. Did that elevator guy bring the dogs out? Reid purposed he was about to find out.

So, he moved behind the cubicles and moved towards their posterior from the other direction. Those three snipers all neared the bloodbath. They access and mobilize in search of the missing Reid. The elevator door closed and reopened. Multiple rounds rained in that direction; one struck the Elevator Serviceman who attempting to recalibrate the seized elevator. Meanwhile, Reid found cover during that onslaught. He worked his way to the roof aided by a dangling rope which the snipers used to let themselves down. Landing on that top floor, Reid boarded that waiting helicopter and took off oblivious to them all.

They prowled in search of Reid in vain. In the meantime, they immediately notified Hobbs of the status on that top floor.

"He's MIA"

Said the lead sniper.

Alternatively, on the ground level, Hobbs informed: "The elevator is now functional! Who's piloting that helicopter that just headed south?" There was no answer.

Returning to the roof, the snipers realized their helicopter was gone. They saw it disappear in the distance.

THE N Y CONNIVERS SERIES

Meanwhile, Jamie Johnson fresh on the scene, joined Hobbs as they board the elevator. Other NYPD officers also took the ride to the top. The door opened and the wounded Elevator Serviceman crawled towards Hobbs and handed him a document. Hobbs folded the paper and placed it inside his breast pocket, and jets to the roof. NYPD officers pacified the Serviceman, bleeding severely. In the intervening time, another helicopter circles. It then touches down on the MSG landing pad.

THE N Y CONNIVERS SERIES

28

Hobbs and Johnson swiftly arrived at the MSG landing pad and briskly boarded the copter. It takes off in the same direction that Clifton Reid's traveled.

In the backdrop, NYPD officers and Medics clean up the mess at the MSG top floor. Hobbs and Johnson received confirmation from Amtrak officials that the train with Tillerson at the helm would be derailed at the Albany station.

THE N Y CONNIVERS SERIES

That's it! To them, this was great news as they can not only now focus their attention on pursuing Clifton Reid but knowledgeably pursue his partner in crime Monica Tillerson as well.

In their pursuit, the information provided by the FAA claimed Reid's helicopter had disappeared from under their radar.

This covertness frustrated the heck out of the two detectives. More so with Hobbs, who worked tirelessly on structuring a deal with Reid before he fled the hostage scene at MSG.

Yet, Hobbs' helicopter remained airborne; just in case Reid's helicopter resurfaced.

In the meantime, the phone rings inside Reid's attorney's office. Trevor Sparks, Brooklyn's

.

"In the air. You won't need them. Right now, just focus on my family." Responds Reid.

"I can't help you if you intend to remain vague with your prospective defense attorney. Do you want my service or not?" Asks Sparks.

"That's why I called, Trevor."

"Where are you? Jamaica? Have you already cleared International Air space? If you are in Jamaica, that's okay. The US could have problems extraditing you." States Sparks.

THE N Y CONNIVERS SERIES

"Trevor, I'm a US citizen, remember? I swore to uphold the constitution." Says Reid.
"That's right but right now you are not. You sat on this for too long, Clifton. Anyway, go ahead. What's your request?" Asks Sparks.
"I need you to look out for my wife and kids. While you are at it, find out what's going on with Rick Tillerson." States Reid.
"If I'm hearing you correctly, please don't do an Anthony Bourdain on us or a Jeffrey Epstein. That's not the right approach to this dilemma. Why don't you just turn yourself in? That way I don't end up in a crossfire." States Sparks.
"Never! I won't. Me, giving in? Says I'm a coward."
Says Reid.
"Why not?"
Asks Sparks.
"I have some unfinished business to undertake."
Says Reid after which he looks himself squarely in the mirror and hangs up the phone.

THE N Y CONNIVERS SERIES

29

Meanwhile, the train continued speedily on its route towards Albany with the Rhinecliff station in its rearview. The two discombobulated couples onboard became more concerning to authorities. Evident by a Police helicopter trailing overhead and dangling a net. Inside the Amtrak office in Albany, operators are discombobulated. Two trains sit on opposite tracks

inside the station. "We need that northbound track clear!" Shouts one of the operators.

"I thought we were derailing the runaway before its arrival. I mean between Rhinecliff and Albany." Says an on-the-ground station operator.

"You've got to be kidding me! One thing goes wrong, and that runaway demolishes the entire station. I'm afraid you are not thinking on your feet. Let's get 449 out of there ASAP."

"You got it!" Says the Ground Operator.

Moments later, train 449 is hauled away to one of the train yard's reserve tracks to accommodate the runaway derailment after it arrives. "Station Op, I'm from the Railroad safety campaign. How many crossings between Rhinecliff and Albany?" "The last time I checked there were ten." "Darn! Ten? The last two were dysfunctional. Luckily, there were no crossers."

"Those remaining eight, run through highly populated residential neighborhoods."

"Darn, this could run into rush hour traffic." "Not only that. School buses could still be making their drop-offs. It's Monday and now after-school hours are upon us. How are we going to manage this?"

Asks the Amtrak Operator. "Where does that one-lane track end?" Asks the Railway Inspector.

THE N Y CONNIVERS SERIES

"I thought we were dealing with those crossings?" Asks the Amtrak Operator. "We are dealing with both probabilities." Says the Railroad Inspector.
"Right after crossing number six. Do you copy?"
"I'm afraid we've got bad news. There's a freight train headed southbound and loaded with hydrochloric acid. It has priority over that main line." Says the Railroad Inspector.
"Where did that tornado originate? Canada? Acid? Did
I hear you say acid?"
Asks the Amtrak Operator.
"That's what they are telling me."
"Where is it now?"
Asks the Amtrak Operator.
"South of Albany and north of Rhinecliff." Replies the rattled Railroad Inspector.
"Holy smokes! Why would the MTA wish this demon on us? For all, we've been to them. These tracks will disintegrate like ashes against the wind. Rhinecliff? Will they both intersect?" Asks the Amtrak Operator.
"It's your guess."
He continues.
"At the speed, this freight train is coming. There's at least a three-minute passage chasm." Says the Railroad inspector.

THE N Y CONNIVERS SERIES

He continues:
"We are now collaborating with local authorities. We'll need to secure those remaining six railroad crossings as well as hoping these two trains don't ever collide."
"Hope?"
Asks the Amtrak Operator.
"Yes. Hope. Neither you nor I have any way of either stopping or slowing down any of those trains. That freight train is more than a mile long. Unless by the waving of some magic wand. It could cross that fork in two minutes and thirty seconds at its current speed. Unless that runaway train speeds up we'll be in good shape. If not, we are screwed! Let's keep our fingers crossed."
Says the Railroad Inspector.
"I'm tired of crossing my fingers since this all began."
Says the Amtrak Operator.

THE N Y CONNIVERS SERIES

30

At the next upcoming railroad crossing, multiple vehicles are sidelined due to a dysfunctional signal. A law enforcement officer instructs motorists to remain in their vehicles until this Amtrak runaway crosses. In the meantime, no signal lights or crossing bells alert, any. Two speeding cars involved in a chase become unstoppable and cross the tracks. They are inevitably demolished.

THE N Y CONNIVERS SERIES

The Amtrak train is slowed slightly in its path.

The community is raveled. Now seen on TV, the Operators at the Albany Station are discombobulated eyeing additional pending danger on this train's route. The news spins unfavorably for the train line. The media is not only spun when and how this train service dilemma all began but also when and how it might all end. This normal civil community has by now seen and experienced too much in the last few hours. Helicopters continue to trail this runaway with Monica Tillerson at the helm. Over some loud audio, Tillerson from their cockpit is warned regarding not only her surrender but the impending danger up ahead per the oncoming freight train. Tillerson remains noncommittal. Although seeing those displayed dangers up ahead signs waving at her at that last crossing. Meanwhile, one helicopter drops a net for those two couples on the train. In multiple succession, they are rescued.

Monica Tillerson hears the horn from the freight train in the distance. She whimpers as the freight train finally bears down approaching the fork up ahead. Her train is doing 85 MPH in a 75 MPH zone. The freight train is doing 90 MPH.

The freight train is now at runaway speed. It's horn crescendo. Albany Operators juggle phone lines

THE N Y CONNIVERS SERIES

wondering if this tornado will clear their train. Both trains are nearing that fork. The freight train's horn crescendo. The Amtrak train's caboose clips the last car of that freight train. Luckily, it only toted a mud bike.

THE N Y CONNIVERS SERIES

31

With the runaway train just a few miles south of Albany Station. Monica Tillerson's cell phone rings. She IDs the caller. It's a familiar number by that smirk on her face. Monica answers spontaneously.

"Clifton, where the hell are you?"

"I'm up above!"

Reid responds.

THE N Y CONNIVERS SERIES

"You mean, you are in Heaven already? I'm still down here fighting Satan and his wicked angels." Tillerson responds.

"No. Look up! I'm in the copter."
Says Reid.

"I've seen so many of them... I can't trust anyone. Even on the inside. Another Insider?" Says Tillerson.

"You are so jaded."
Responds Reid.

"I'm dropping a net for you to climb up."

"What do I need a net for? I'm not a fish. My name is Monica. Not Robin the fish nor the bird." Tillerson responds.

"Monica. If you know what I know, you will catch this net and get off that train. It's dangling to your right."
Says Reid authoritatively.

"Cliff, I don't need a net. I'm heading to Springfield, Massachusetts, and I know how to get there. My peeps are waiting for me with a prepared bunker."
Says Tillerson.

"I don't want to treat you like a fish or a chick. However, you are missing the boat, Tillerson. They are planning to derail the train you are sitting comfortably in. At your next stop, Albany which is

THE N Y CONNIVERS SERIES

a few miles up ahead. You need to get off that death mobile."
Says Reid.
"My destination is Springfield. I have promises to keep."
Responds Tillerson.
"Yeah. But you won't make
"Cliff, I will. That switch at Albany will malfunction. They always do. Remember the 'Unstoppable?'
Says Tillerson.
"You have not been watching the news. If it doesn't that crossing at the Boston/Chicago fork is littered with law enforcement. They are set to derail it manually at that intersection if Albany fails." Says Reid.
"I don't think they will put themselves in harm's way. Springfield baby!" Says Tillerson.
"You should have watched the news." "There is no TV up in here." Responds Tillerson.
"There are Apps for Cable channels on your smartphone."
"Cliff, you know I've always owned a razor 'a flip' what do you call that, a dumbphone? Well, I still own it. Those smarties are way too expensive for me."
Meanwhile, the net dangles invitingly.

THE N Y CONNIVERS SERIES

"Stop playing around, Monica. In a few moments, the air above you could be littered with cops in helicopters. Then you won't hear me any longer. Do you know the train you are on has no brakes, and that all its brake fluid leaked out at Penn Station? You want to see your son alive again, don't you? They have been talking bad about you all over the news. Saying 'You might not even be aware you are driving a runaway train.' That means you are dumb. Just like your darn phone. Dumb!"
Says Reid.
"Move that net closer to the front. Closer to the right. Now have it touch the train. Gently now!" Says Tillerson, after which she climbs out. Grabs it and is airborne.
Onboard, they high-five each other. With not much time to celebrate, the train speeds non-stop through Albany station. Before it diverted to the run-off tracks. The woman last seen at Penn Station toting her defective luggage waves from the last train car. Fleeing the area, they notice the derailment and massive explosion while their helicopter speeds away.

THE N Y CONNIVERS SERIES

32

Reid and Tillerson share hard looks.
"See?"
Asks Reid.
"Why don't you finish you rebuke…See I told you so?"
Asks Tillerson.
"I did. Now we need to clear this airspace and hopefully fly under the radar."

THE N Y CONNIVERS SERIES

"You mean, they are still after you? By the way, how did you pull all this off?"

"It's not over until it's over, Monica."

"You never told me you knew how to fly?"

Asked Tillerson.

"You've never asked." Says

Reid.

There's significant silence amongst them. "Life is like a mystery most times. If we knew everything before it happened. Life would be a constant scare." Says Reid.

"You are right. Life is very uncanny. It is. Never driven an Amtrak train before. They do run faster, smoother, and better than those subway trains. Their speed limit is much higher, Cliff. Kind of wished they were as high as those bullet trains in Europe…320 MPH. I would have already arrived in Springfield, Massachusetts. Hang out with my homies. So, how did you pull this off?" Asks Tillerson.

"Greater is He that is in us than he that is in the world." Replies Reid.

"So, where are you going, to Jamaica?"

Asks Tillerson.

"My Yard."

Says Reid.

THE N Y CONNIVERS SERIES

Suddenly, they are tailed by multiple law-enforcement choppers. Inside the lead chopper, Hobbs, and Johnson command:
"Reid you need to land this helicopter for your safety."
Says Hobbs over the radio.
"Not a chance!"
Says Reid in response.
"What if they fly to Jamaica?"
Asks Johnson off the record.
"We'll follow them."
Says Hobbs.
"International Airspace?"
Asks Johnson.
"Coke 'Dudas' was extradited from Jamaica. Plus, Reid's a US citizen."
Says Hobbs.
"Never been there."
Says Johnson.
"Jamaica? Nice place. But let us not even entertain that thought. We wind up there they can make our lives a living hell. The US might have to go to war to get us out. Not another Grenada."
"Why? They protect their own?"
Asks Johnson.
"They do. They do…"

THE N Y CONNIVERS SERIES

Says Hobbs.

"You have no idea what I've done before or is capable of?" Says Johnson.

"Let's see you jump out and stop their helicopter. Handcuff Reid and Tillerson and bring them on board…That's pretty farfetched, don't you think? States Hobbs.

"Don't push me. I'm close to the edge and I just might!"

Responds Johnson as she looks down below at the awaiting distance.

THE N Y CONNIVERS SERIES

33

While Reid's helicopter increases its distance ahead of its pursuers. Reid first notices the fuel gauge, and then Tillerson is stuck on E.

"What do we do now? There are no refueling trucks up here."

States Tillerson.

"Something deep down inside told me I should have driven that train to Springfield." She continued.

THE N Y CONNIVERS SERIES

Suddenly, the air is littered with police helicopters in pursuit as they cross over Staten Island airspace and into Brooklyn. Reid begins to whistle. "I don't think they are that generous." Says Tillerson. "Generous?" Asks Reid.
"I mean to bring us fuel. Seeing we are one of them." Says Tillerson.
"We were. Either we descend now while we are still on fumes, or we descend later when we can't choose where to land."
Says Reid. "There's the Canarsie Pier!" Says Tillerson.
Moments later, the helicopter lands. Bullets scatter in their direction from pursuing helicopters with nowhere to land.

TILLERSON APPROACHES a stud in a parked Mustang.
"Police business! We need to borrow your car.
They board very quickly.
"I've envisioned this. After shooting those hostages at GCT. Now, this is for real. Buckle up! It's the law in Brooklyn. You should know that."
Says Tillerson, strapped under the driver's wheel.
Reid complies.
They attempt their getaway via the Belt Parkway.

THE N Y CONNIVERS SERIES

34

Headed east is traffic-laden. The stolen Mustang with Tillerson at the wheel weaves through crowded lanes, gaining access in its path. NTPD helicopters hover overhead. Back at the pier, several cars clear the

THE N Y CONNIVERS SERIES

parking lot to accommodate landing for Hobbs and Johnson's helicopter. An NYPD officer shows up pronto with a black sedan. They jump in and take off. The pursuing black sedan replicates those traffic maneuvers. The sign for the Pennsylvania Avenue exit looms in dark green with milk-white lettering.

The Mustang exits in runaway mode. The upcoming street sign says Cozine Avenue. Tillerson takes it. The black sedan bears down with a flashing red light on its dashboard. In it, Detective Jamie Johnson helms Detective Jonathan Hobbs as a passenger.

From the helicopter up above:

"Mustang just turned left onto

Cozine." "That's a copy!" Says

Johnson.

The Sedan tails playing catchup on this street with very few traffic lights.

The Mustang hits a speedbump and Reid's head almost hits the roof. He's shaken up and stares over at Tillerson with a disciplinary look.

"Do you want to be dropped off at your yard?" Asks Tillerson.

There's silence.

Suddenly, Reid replies.

"We are in this thing together. That's why I came to get you from that runaway train."

THE N Y CONNIVERS SERIES

The traffic light changes from yellow to red. Tillerson takes the light speeding up drastically. Reverting to Pennsylvania
Ave. Multiple law enforcement cars now join the pursuing convoy. Yet, Tillerson wouldn't let up. Jamie Johnson is close on her tail with Hobbs looking for the perfect aim at the rear tires. He shoots and misses.

Tillerson speeds up and merges onto the Jackie Robinson Parkway, a winding, curvy stretch of roadway. The chase ensues erratically. Signs for the Grand Central Parkway, Whitestone Bridge, and Long Island Expressway all beckon. Tillerson, with Johnson on the Mustang's tail, again has to choose quickly. She takes the Grand Central East. Familiar with the streets in Queens, Tillerson opts and exits on Union Turnpike and continues on the service roadway. The chase continues with other motorists giving the right-away. In the air, NYPD helicopters are in pursuit. A roadblock up ahead and close to Jamaica Estates presents a deterrent for Tillerson. Cleverly she makes a detour rerouting to a 360 and back onto the Grand Central Parkway.

It's a trap as law enforcement has now shut down the flow of eastbound traffic on GCP East. Multiple helicopters have taken up residence on the parkway.

THE N Y CONNIVERS SERIES

Hobbs and Johnson dart out of their sedan armed with doors still ajar.
"Drop your weapons and come out of the car slowly with hands above your head!" Says Hobbs.
In the backdrop, defense lawyer Trevor Sparks arrives.
"I'm the attorney for the defense!"
He yells.
On the front seat of Sparks' car is Rick Tillerson the son of Monica Tillerson.
Tillerson, with a smirk on her face at the sight of Rick, exits followed by Reid. Cops surround and place them in handcuffs. And confiscates two packages of computer chips from the automobile.

THE N Y CONNIVERS SERIES

About The AUTHOR

John Alan Andrews hails from the islands of SVG in the Caribbean. He began his acting career in New York. In 1996 he took his craft to Hollywood. He appeared in multiple TV Ads campaigns, and films including John Q, starring Denzel Washington. Andrews later found his niche - writing coupled with filmmaking, and not only starred in but produced and directed some of his work which won multiple awards in Hollywood.

With over 76 books in his multi-genre catalog, including **Rude Buay** poised for a Jamaican production, Andrews is currently drafting **The PIPS Series,** which is a police procedural TV series slated for the Mediterranean enclaves. He has also Co-Authored with his sons **Jonathan Andrews** and **Jefferri Andrews**.

His latest books **Atomic Steps** and **Make Every Thought Pay You A Profit** are favs among business leaders, and his twisted **NYC Connivers** legal thriller series appeals to both women and men ages 16 -85. **The Pips Series (Body in A Suitcase)**. Also, **Samuel A. Andrews - Legacy** (A Biography).

More of his work can be found at **ALIPNET.COM** or **ALIPNET TV,** his recently launched OTT Streaming Platform.

John Alan Andrews states:

"Some people create, while others compete. Creating is where the rubber meets the road. A dream worth having is one worth fighting for because freedom is not free; it carries a massive price tag."

THE N Y CONNIVERS SERIES

THE N Y CONNIVERS SERIES

THE N Y CONNIVERS SERIES

THE N Y CONNIVERS SERIES

THE N Y CONNIVERS SERIES

THE N Y CONNIVERS SERIES

THE N Y CONNIVERS SERIES

SAUCE 02:29

A SUSPENSE MYSTERY HORROR

FROM THE CREATOR OF
RUDE BUAY

JOHN ALAN ANDREWS

THE N Y CONNIVERS SERIES

THE N Y CONNIVERS SERIES

THE SOUL OF BLACK WALL STREET

OPTIONED FOR FILM

JOHN ALAN ANDREWS

#1 INTERNATIONAL BESTSELLER

THE N Y CONNIVERS SERIES

THE N Y CONNIVERS SERIES

THE N Y CONNIVERS SERIES

ATOMIC STEPS

WIN BIG OR GO HOME

WARNING: If you are determined to stay in your comfort zone, this book may not be for you.

INTERNATIONAL BESTSELLING AUTHOR
JOHN ALAN ANDREWS

THE N Y CONNIVERS SERIES

THE N Y CONNIVERS SERIES

THE N Y CONNIVERS SERIES

THE N Y CONNIVERS SERIES

THE N Y CONNIVERS SERIES

THE N Y CONNIVERS SERIES

THE N Y CONNIVERS SERIES

THE N Y CONNIVERS SERIES

The FIVE "Ps" FOR TEENS

National Bestselling Author
John A. Andrews

THE N Y CONNIVERS SERIES

THE N Y CONNIVERS SERIES

ANDREWS

John A. Andrews

Author of
"Quotes" Unlimited &
How I Wrote 8 Books In One Year™

THE N Y CONNIVERS SERIES

THE N Y CONNIVERS SERIES

THE N Y CONNIVERS SERIES

THE N Y CONNIVERS SERIES

THE N Y CONNIVERS SERIES

THE N Y CONNIVERS SERIES

THE N Y CONNIVERS SERIES

THE N Y CONNIVERS SERIES

THE N Y CONNIVERS SERIES

THE N Y CONNIVERS SERIES

THE N Y CONNIVERS SERIES

THE N Y CONNIVERS SERIES

THE N Y CONNIVERS SERIES

THE N Y CONNIVERS SERIES

THE UNITED STATES PANDEMIC

FIGHTING THE INVISIBLE ENEMY

JOHN A. ANDREWS

THE AFTERMATH OF COVID – 19

THE N Y CONNIVERS SERIES

JOHN A. ANDREWS

The Church or *A HOSPITAL?*

THE MUSICAL

FROM THE CREATOR OF
RUDE BUAY
THE WHODUNIT CHRONICLES
&
THE CHURCH ON FIRE

SO MANY ARE TRYING TO GO TO HEAVEN
WITHOUT FIRST BUILDING A HEAVEN
HERE ON EARTH...
#1 INTERNATIONAL BESTSELLER

THE N Y CONNIVERS SERIES

THE N Y CONNIVERS SERIES

THE N Y CONNIVERS SERIES

THE N Y CONNIVERS SERIES

CROSS ATLANTIC FIASCO

A Riveting Novel

THREE EX-COPS, THEIR EX-BOSS, HIS 9 YEAR OLD DAUGHTER, AND THE BIGGEST BANK HEIST EVER ORCHESTRATED...

RENEGADE COPS

#1 INTERNATIONAL BESTSELLER

JOHN A. ANDREWS

Creator of
The RUDE BUAY Series
&
The WHODUNIT CHRONICLES

THE N Y CONNIVERS SERIES

THE N Y CONNIVERS SERIES

THE N Y CONNIVERS SERIES

JOHN ALAN ANDREWS

BLACK JUSTICE
A SNITCH ON TIME

THE N Y CONNIVERS SERIES

JOHN & JONATHAN ANDREWS

BLACK JUSTICE

INJUSTICE BAKED IN

THE N Y CONNIVERS SERIES

THE N Y CONNIVERS SERIES

RUDE GIRL

UNEXPECTED SUSPECTS

FROM THE CREATOR OF
RUDE BUAY
JOHN ALAN ANDREWS

THE N Y CONNIVERS SERIES

THE N Y CONNIVERS SERIES

THE N Y CONNIVERS SERIES

THE PIPS®

ALIPNET ORIGINAL

WRITTEN BY
JOHN ALAN ANDREWS

CREATOR OF
RUDE BUAY

THE THUMB DRIVES

THE N Y CONNIVERS SERIES

THE N Y CONNIVERS SERIES

ALIPNET ORIGINAL

THE PIPS®

MANHUNT IN PARADISE

WRITTEN BY

JOHN ALAN ANDREWS

CREATOR OF
RUDE BUAY

THE N Y CONNIVERS SERIES

THE N Y CONNIVERS SERIES

COMING SOON

THE N Y CONNIVERS SERIES

THE N Y CONNIVERS SERIES

THE PIPS®

THE FRENCH CONNECT

WRITTEN BY
JOHN ALAN ANDREWS

CREATOR OF
RUDE BUAY
ALIBNET
ORIGINAL

THE N Y CONNIVERS SERIES

THE PIPS®

ALIPNET
ORIGINAL

WRITTEN BY
JOHN ALAN ANDREWS

CREATOR OF
RUDE BUAY

BAD JOHNNY

THE N Y CONNIVERS SERIES

THE N Y CONNIVERS SERIES

THE N Y CONNIVERS SERIES

ALi™ PICTURES

THE N Y CONNIVERS SERIES

UP ™

UNCANNY PICTURES

THE N Y CONNIVERS SERIES

BOOKS THAT WILL ENHANCE YOUR LIFE

THE N Y CONNIVERS SERIES

ALIPNET
ORIGINAL

THE N Y CONNIVERS SERIES

Made in the USA
Columbia, SC
09 January 2025

178e7d1c-20f9-4956-89c0-1cb66fd933afR01